Josie's
Handful of Quietness

Josie's
Handful of Quietness

Nancy Covert Smith
Drawings by Ati Forberg

ABINGDON PRESS
Nashville
New York

JOSIE'S HANDFUL OF QUIETNESS

Library of Congress Cataloging in Process Data

SMITH, NANCY COVERT.   Josie's handful of quietness
    SUMMARY: Used to the hard life of her migrant family,
twelve-year-old Josie finally realizes her dream of a permanent
home and school.
[1. Migrant labor—Fiction. 2. Friendship—Fiction] I. Title.
PZ7.S6564Jo   [Fic]   74-5024

ISBN 0-687-20560-3

MANUFACTURED BY THE PARTHENON PRESS AT
NASHVILLE, TENNESSEE, UNITED STATES OF AMERICA

To Rosie who found her Handful of Quietness

and to my children
Mark, Leanne, Craig, and Tammy:
May they each find theirs

1

Josie splashed the last of the soapy water from the bucket onto the kitchen floor. Sitting back on her heels, she swiped her long black hair from her sweaty cheeks and smiled at Maria and Carlos. Her baby brother and little sister sat cross-legged on the table, watching her, yet out of her way.

Maria pulled her two sucking fingers from her mouth, "We get down now, Josie?"

"Not yet. I still have to rinse. It will not take long. This floor is old. It slants so the water runs out the back door without my help."

Josie bent back to her job of trying to scrub away years of cooking grease from the bare gray boards. The job was too hard for a twelve-year-old girl.

Carlos should have been in bed for his nap.

The only reason he was not crying was because she had already given him his midday bottle. He sucked peacefully, his brown cheeks pumping, his round black eyes following her movements on the floor.

Maria's small chest swelled to push out a big sigh of boredom.

Josie smiled, "I will hurry, Maria. Just watch Carlos a little longer. If you do, I will play ball outside with you while he is sleeping. OK?"

"*Sí*," Maria cried with a quick smile. She flopped on her belly and slid from the table. "I will find the ball."

"Maria!" Josie reached to grab her sister, but Maria was already running out the door. Josie called after her, "I told you, watch Carlos!"

Behind Josie a crash. Then the baby's screams. Josie twisted to find Carlos facedown on the floor. A stream of milk followed the rinse water out the back door.

"Oh, Carlos." Josie bent to pick him up. Then she saw the milk stream turning pink as blood from somewhere joined the current. "Oh, Carlos, *niño pequeño* . . . baby." Quickly she turned him over. Under him lay the shattered bottle. Blood smeared together with tears and dirt on his face.

8

He fought Josie with frightened, flailing fists. "Ahhhhhh . . ."

"Shush. *Quieto.* Let me see."

The baby only doubled his efforts. "Ahhhhh . . ."

Josie felt tears sting her own eyes. "Don't cry. Don't cry." She did not know if the words were for herself or Carlos.

Maria had come back to stand in the doorway, her fingers stuck in her mouth, her eyes wide with fright.

Josie yelled at her above the baby's screams. "It is your fault. Bad girl. You ran away."

Maria's face twisted as she began to cry. "Maria sorry."

"It is too late for sorry now."

Maria ran to Josie and flung herself against Josie's back. "I am sorry." Carlos screamed in her arms. What should she do? There was no one but her. No one to ask. No one to help.

If only the children would be quiet, perhaps then she could think. If only her mother were home instead of working the field. If only she knew someone here in Ohio. But who was there?

Then she thought of the farm down the road. There must be someone there. Yes, she would go see.

Standing up, she dragged the end of her

T-shirt across Carlos' face to wipe away some of the blood and dirt. Then, holding Carlos on her hip with one arm and pulling Maria after her with the other hand, she pushed backward out the screen door. Carefully, she helped Maria down the broken step on the porch before urging her into a run. The road was a one-lane blacktop. She dropped Maria's hand, so she could hold the struggling baby with both arms. "Run now. Keep up."

Maria needed no encouragement. The hot tar on the road made her pick up her bare feet quickly. To the rhythm of their running she chanted, "I am sorry, Josie. I am sorry."

At first Josie did not hear her. She was busy scanning the field across the road for signs of her mother, even though she knew she was in the east field planting today. But finally, when she stopped to shift Carlos to the other side, Maria's cries broke through to her. Maria's turned up face quivered so pitifully, Josie tugged one of the black braids and said, "It is OK."

Once forgiven, Maria quieted to soft sobs as they began to run again.

Since the two houses were separated by a huge orchard, they had been running past rows and rows of apple trees. Now, as they came to the end of the grove of trees, Josie cut

10

across the gravel driveway and through the front yard. She felt soft grass under her shoes and noticed pink flowers, but she could not take time to look at them or to think about the strangers who lived here. If she did, she could not be so bold as to ask for help.

She half dragged, half helped Maria up the porch steps. Their feet thudded down the long wooden porch. Carlos' screams worked like a doorbell. Already the door was opening and a man was reaching out.

Gratefully, Josie gave up her heavy load and followed the man into a big white kitchen. Out of habit, she pulled Maria to her to keep her out of trouble.

The man did not ask questions. He put the baby on the counter, searching to find the source of the blood. Carlos had grown tired, so his cries had begun to weaken. The man was able to investigate the swollen lip. Opening a drawer, he took a clean dish towel, wet the edge of it under the cold water faucet, and gently placed it on Carlos' face. Crooning in a deep rumbly voice, he tilted his head to look through the lower part of his bifocals. "Hey, fella, what happened to you? Take a fall did you? Well, it doesn't seem to be too bad. A little ice should fix you up."

For the first time the old man seemed to

notice Josie and Maria. "Girl, look in the refrigerator freezer and get me some ice."

Josie set Maria firmly on a chair and walked to the big square refrigerator on the other side of the kitchen.

"Give the handle a stout pull, girl, or it won't open. Getting old and reluctant to work, like me."

Josie tugged the door open and found the ice cube tray. The man wrapped a piece of the ice in the dishcloth. He set Carlos up and supported him with his arm while he applied the cold to the puffy lip.

The emergency past, the man slowly looked the girls over from head to toe.

Josie felt the squishiness of her sneakers, knew her cutoff jeans were damp from the mopping, and that her T-shirt was blood-stained and dirty. Not a very good impression to make on this neighbor they had just met. Her hands smoothed Maria's mussed braids.

"Don't think I know you children. You from the camp?"

"No. Well, yes."

"You sound confused."

Josie lifted her chin and set her shoulders straight. She had been asked questions like this before and did not like them. "I mean, yes, my mother and father, they work in the

12

fields, but no, we do not live in the camp. We live in the house on the other side of your orchard."

"The old Miller place. Mr. Welter rent it to you?"

Josie did not like strangers who asked questions, but this man had been good to Carlos, so she had better be polite. "Yes, my father likes our family to be alone."

"I often wondered how Roy Welter decided who got the houses and who got the shacks when you migrants arrive for the summer."

At the word migrant Josie looked down at her dirty sneakers. She did not like being called a migrant in that way. They were Mexican-American farm laborers. This man said migrant in a way that made it undesirable.

The old man must have noticed her resentment, because he said, "No offense. It's just that so many of my apples get stolen by your people. I wouldn't mind the windfalls, but when the workers pull them off the trees before they're ripe and then throw them on the ground, I don't like it. That's waste. I work hard to make a living."

Josie just said, "If Carlos is all right, we will go now."

"Oh, he's all right. More frightened than anything. There's a cut on his lip, and it's going to stay swollen for awhile, but I don't think it needs stitches."

Josie picked the baby up. "Thank you."

She felt the man's hand on her shoulder. "I hurt your feelings, didn't I?"

"It does not matter."

"Sure it matters. I'm an old man who talks before he thinks. I had no right to lump all you people together and call you all thieves."

Josie stared straight ahead.

"Just a minute." The man shuffled out to a back porch. Josie noticed he had a limp. One leg was stiff. He came back with three popsicles. "Remembered I had these in the big freezer. Make your brother's mouth feel cool. He'll like it better than the plain ice."

"No, thank you. You have already done enough."

"Don't be pigheaded, girl. I'm trying to say I'm sorry." He unwrapped the red treat and handed it to Carlos. The baby leaned forward eagerly, holding out his hands. When the man stooped to hand one to Maria, Josie looked sternly at the little girl, but the temptation was too much. Maria looked away from Josie and smiled at the man. She took the popsicle and said politely, *"Gracias."*

14

Josie firmly refused hers. The old man grunted and took it for himself. "Come on, we'll eat them on the porch swing. Then the drips won't matter."

Josie could see there was nothing she could do but follow the man out the door. The man took Maria into his lap as soon as they sat down on the swing. She went gladly. A red popsicle was all it took to win *her* as a friend.

Carlos soon forgot about his accident. As the swing swayed, he relaxed against Josie's chest. His eyelids drooped, and he stopped licking the melting popsicle and started sucking it like a nipple. She felt a stream of sticky cherry juice drip off his elbow onto her knee.

The old man talked to Maria. "Can you tell me your name?"

Maria ducked her head shyly. "Maria."

"Maria what?"

"García."

"Maria García. That is an *elegant* name."

Maria giggled at the sound of the strange word. She leaned her head against the man's chest.

"And how old are you, Maria García?"

Maria giggled again.

Josie slapped at the little girl's brown leg. "It is not nice to laugh at people. Politely answer the man's question."

15

Maria held up four fingers, then said soberly, "You rumble inside when you talk." She put her ear back on the man's chest and said, "Talk, please."

The man laughed and squeezed Maria tightly to him.

Josie watched them and thought, Maybe I have been too cross. Maybe I have not been fair. She said, "My name is Josie."

The man held out his hand to her like she was an adult. "Glad to meet you, Josie. My name is Glenn Curtis."

They swung a few minutes in silence.

Thinking she should make conversation, she asked, "Do you live here alone?"

Mr. Curtis cleared his throat. Josie saw his chin begin to quiver in just the way Maria's had after Carlos' fall. When he looked at her, his faded blue eyes were full of a great sadness. "I've lived alone for over a year now. Mary, my wife, died a year ago spring just before the apple blossoms came on. She always liked blossom time. Washed the dishes looking out the window at them. When the wind blew and the petals dropped, she said it looked like a shower of snow in the spring. 'Come see them, Glenn,' she would call, as if I didn't see enough of them working in the orchard every day."

He stopped talking. Josie thought he had gotten lost in his memories. She sat quietly. Carlos dropped to sleep, and Maria was being lulled by the swing to follow him. She and the old man were alone, held together by the weight of the sleeping children.

What could she say to this man who lived alone in a big house with a big white kitchen where popsicles were kept for everyday treats? She could think of nothing else, so she said, "You have pretty flowers."

"My peonies? You like flowers, eh? Wait till this summer when my marigolds bloom. Yellow flowers everywhere. I'll give you some to plant in your yard."

Josie thought of the small square of packed down dirt on either side of the cracked sidewalk that was supposed to be their front yard. In one corner a trumpet vine wound around the wire fence. In the other corner deep ruts from their truck discouraged even weeds from growing. She shook her head. "I do not think they will grow anywhere in our yard."

"Sure they will, if I show you how. You see, I save the seeds each fall after the flowers die. Then, in the spring I broadcast them in every direction. All up and down the ditch banks. The strong ones take root, grow, and bloom.

You wait and see, Josie García, marigolds'll bloom for you, too."

Mr. Curtis smiled at her. Slowly she smiled back.

Abruptly she remembered her manners. "I should go now. You have things to do, and I must start the supper so Mama can finish it when she comes home."

"I don't have anything to do, Josie. It doesn't take much for one person to get along. I'll walk you home. You carry Carlos and I'll bring Maria. Then they can stay asleep."

Josie stood up and jostled Carlos until she could carry him comfortably. She waited until Mr. Curtis got stiffly to his feet.

On the road she adjusted her walk to his limp. Quietly, so they would not disturb the little ones, they talked. He pointed out the various kinds of trees to her as they passed the rows of the orchard. "Red Delicious . . . Grimes Golden . . . Jonathan . . . Stayman Red . . ."

Josie thought, What a beautiful place. I would like to watch the apples ripen. Next spring I would like to see the apple blossoms from *my* kitchen window.

But then they came to the end of the orchard and she saw the house where she lived.

20

An unpainted, rundown house like all the other houses she had lived in. A place to stay just long enough to get in a crop and move on. This was the first of June. Sometime in September they would pack and be on their way south and west searching for a winter crop. It was foolish of her to think of apple orchards and planting marigolds. She was a migrant, a mover. She didn't belong any-where.

2

With the children asleep, Josie bent back over the kitchen floor. Carefully she picked up the pieces of glass, resoaked the milk, and scrubbed away the stains. Rubbing her hands on the back of her jeans, she looked around their kitchen. Not much like Mr. Curtis' large one. Theirs held a wooden table, two chairs and a bench, a small icebox, and a three-burner hotplate. Two wooden cupboards on the wall had doors that either stuck or didn't stay shut, depending on whether the day was rainy or dry. A water bucket and dipper sat on a small shelf, and a calendar from Martin's Feedstore hung on the wall.

The living room wasn't much more comfortable. Along its walls stood two more chairs like the ones in the kitchen, a dark table with chipped varnish, and a broken-down couch that smelled like a baby's diapers. The furniture had come with the house. They only brought with them cooking pans, blankets, clothes, Carlos' crib, some chipped plates, and other odds and ends.

Upstairs, two rooms tried to fit under the sloping roof. One was a bedroom for their father and mother and Carlos, the other for her and Maria.

Josie cleared away the bucket and scrub rag and thought about supper. She would try to make it a good one tonight. Mother and Father would come home tired. Planting was hard work.

The truck with the tomato plants had arrived yesterday at Mr. Welter's barns. They were bunched in peat moss under wet burlap. Josie knew from other farms that all day her father had been driving the transplanting machine. Behind him, two men would feed the plants down the trough, so each plant fell into the watered row. But it was her mother whose back would ache. Her mother followed the planter; stooping, holding the plant up straight, patting the loose dirt around the plant, walking on to the next one. She never had time to straighten except at the end of a long row. Always she walked in slow rhythm,

23

the sun on her back, the mud caked on her hands, drying and pulling at her skin.

Josie slammed a frying pan onto the hot plate. She would fry the *tortillas*. She would not think about how hard they worked on other men's farms. That kind of thinking made her hurt inside.

She would wash the windows. If her mother would not let her help in the fields, then she would keep the house clean so her mother would not have to get up early to do so much. As Josie rubbed the kitchen window with a piece of crumpled newspaper, she wondered if her mother had ever seen the blossoms on an apple tree in the spring. They did not need the calendar from Martin's Feedstore. They counted time by strawberries to pick, sugar beets to hoe, tomatoes to plant. Angrily Josie flipped the *tortillas*, wondering what she could cook to put on them.

Later Josie sat on the porch steps trying to keep Carlos from eating dirt from the ground. Maria had climbed up three rows on the wire fence to watch for their parents. It bowed as she swung back and forth waiting. During planting and harvest, the two children saw little of their parents. Josie was their substitute.

Maria called out, "Mama is coming."

The mother's face broke into a smile as she waved her straw hat, calling out, *"Niños . . .* children."

The little ones ran to her.

When they were all seated at the supper table, Josie told her parents all about Carlos' accident and how kind Mr. Curtis had been to them.

Maria added her word to the story, "Popsicle."

"Was it good, *muchacha?"* Mrs. García asked.

"Sí," Maria smiled and nodded her head until her black braids bounced.

Mr. García checked Carlos' mouth. "Popsicle seems to be good medicine."

When Josie had hung the dish towels on the fence to dry, she came up on the front porch. Mrs. García sat with her feet on the top step, her head lying forward on her knees. Josie knelt behind her mother to rub the tired muscles in her neck and shoulders. "Let me work for you tomorrow, Mother. I do not mind following the planter."

Mrs. García patted Josie's hand as it massaged her shoulder. "No, Josie. You stay in the house, out of the fields. You do not want hands like mine."

Josie looked at her mother's scarred, calloused, and stained hands. Since her mother was ten years old, she had worked in the fields. She had gone to school only when she could be spared. Josie's grandparents had come up from Mexico in a truck when her mother was a baby. There had been so many riding in the back, they had to stand up to make room. The United States would make them rich, they had been told. It had only made the grandmother twisted with rheumatism, the grandfather a slave to whiskey, and a field hand out of their daughter.

Mrs. García sighed, "No, *muchacha,* do not go to the fields or they will own your soul. You go to school. Someday you will have a *good* job."

Josie sat down on the step.

Together they enjoyed the silence of the early evening. Mrs. García asked, "You like this man, Mr. Curtis, so much?"

"I think so. At first he sounded like the others, not wanting us here because we are migrants. But he is different. This man loves. I know by the way he keeps the house clean to remember his wife, by the way he talks of his orchard, by the way he plants flowers and by the way he helped Carlos."

"He sounds like a busy man. You will not bother this Mr. Curtis too much."

26

"He is lonely too, Mama."

"Why should a man with so much be lonely?"

"I do not know all the reason for his sadness, but his eyes see something they do not want to see, I think."

Night came closer. From the house rippled Carlos' laughter as he bounced on his father's knees. Maria joined them on the porch to lean tiredly on her mother's lap, her sucking fingers pushed into her mouth, listening to her mother's soft comforting voice.

Mrs. García pointed out the wishing star.

Josie made a wish on it, then asked, "Mama, was there ever something you wanted very much when you were young like me?"

Mrs. García was quiet a long time, looking again at her rough hands. When she finally did speak it was only to say, "It has been too long to remember. But you, Josie, you are young. Your life is ahead of you. Do you have dreams?"

Josie hesitated. Should she say her dream out loud? It was what she just wished on the evening star. What she wished on every evening star. Would not telling it destroy any chance of making it come true? But the wanting to share it was so big, she could not keep from telling it. "Yes, Mama, I want to stay

27

here. I do not want to move anymore. I want to go to only one school. I want to belong to a place like Mr. Curtis belongs to his." There was no use stopping now. She went on, "I want to go to college someday, to be a teacher. This year I will be in 7th grade. In one school I could make high grades, high enough for a scholarship. My teacher in Florida, this spring, said I could if I really want to. And I want to, Mama. I really do."

Josie stopped. She could not believe she had actually said all those things out loud. Shocked at herself, she looked up at her mother to see what she was going to do.

Her mother said nothing, only looked at her hands.

But behind them Josie heard her father say, "So you do not like the life I give you?"

Josie whirled to find her father standing above her, his black eyes hard, his hand doubled into a fist pulled back to explode in anger.

"No, Father, I did not . . ."

"I do not give you diamonds for your fingers, eh, my princess?"

Josie felt her mother's hand touch her shoulder. Heard her mother's soft voice pleading, "Ramón, it is only a girl's dream. Do you not dream some days?"

28

"I have no time for dreaming. I work hard like a man should. Only those who are lazy have the time to dream dreams. Put Josie in the fields. Let the sun burn out the fairy stories in her head. Let her back ache like ours, Eva. Let her earn her way."

Josie felt her mother's grip tighten, felt herself pushed aside. Her mother stood straight in front of her husband, her own eyes blazing black. "Josie is not lazy. She is a good girl."

"Get out of the way, Eva. Do not interfere between my daughter and me." Josie saw her father reach to loosen his belt.

Her mother shoved her toward the door. "Josie, take Maria upstairs."

Josie grabbed the little girl, who was already sobbing because of the fighting, and held her head safely in the curve of her neck. As she hurried into the house, she heard her father yell, "You want Josie's beating, do you, Eva?"

Then the sickening sound of flesh striking flesh. Her mother moaned. Josie fled up the stairs to the hot, stuffy bedroom.

As she undressed Maria and sat her on the potty, Josie let tears wash her own face. She could still hear the sound of the slap her mother took in her place. How foolish she was to tell her dream out loud. What trouble it caused.

As she helped Maria into her nightgown, the little girl patted her cheek, "Do not cry, Josie."

"Oh, Maria, I am a bad girl."

Maria kissed her. "Josie not bad. I love Josie."

Josie laid the child down on the bed next to the wall, then crawled in beside her.

"Josie, you are still dressed."

"I know. I will stay a minute. Shush now, go to sleep."

Josie lay quietly. Downstairs it was silent. The fighting was over. Why did she not go downstairs? Why did she lay here hiding? The day slipped completely into night. The room darkened. Josie's tears and the day's hard work urged her to sleep.

It was much later that the sound of voices in the next bedroom wakened her.

"This old man puts foolish notions in Josie's head?"

"No, Ramón. Josie burst tonight like a tomato that lies too long in the sun. She has been thinking this dream long, I am sure."

"I do not understand this, Eva."

"Times are changing, Ramón. Josie sees this. She learns the new ways in the school."

30

"Then we should keep her at home."

"No, our children, they will search for a new way, a way different than ours."

Josie heard noises of her father moving about the room. "I cannot sleep. The room, it is too hot. I will walk." Josie heard him cross the room and then shuffle to a stop. "Eva, I know only our way."

"I know."

A small silence and then he said, "Eva, I am sorry I hit you."

"I know."

Josie waited until her father had gone down the steps and out into the night, then she got quietly off the bed and began undressing. As she stood at the window, she saw her father's shadow moving in the moonlight. Always he was sorry after he struck them. She understood and could not be bitter. He could not talk well like her mother. When he was worried, his mind seemed to close up so he could only speak with his fists.

They could not stay here. She could not speak again of college. There would be no marigolds. Josie lay down again beside Maria and put her arm around the little girl. In her sleep Maria sighed and rolled close. Josie covered them both with the sheet. The spring night was beginning to turn cool.

3

The tomato planting was finished. Carlos' lip was healing. Josie continued her job as substitute mother. The days were much the same, filled with work and the children and otherwise being alone. She wished often for someone to talk to.

One morning the sun groped its way through the window to waken her, and she lay blinking against its brightness. As she collected her thoughts for the day, she remembered that on her walk back from Mr. Curtis' place the day of the accident, he had pointed out wild asparagus growing. After breakfast dishes and washing Carlos' diapers, she would walk to the spot on the ditch bank and see if there might be enough stalks to pick for supper.

With Carlos on her hip and Maria by her side, they went out into the quiet morning. Only Maria's chattering and the sound of a cardinal broke the stillness. The country was such a silent place to live, she thought, especially when you knew no one except your family.

Workers were bent over in a distant field, replanting by hand the spots where the first tomatoes, machine planted, had not survived the shock of transplant. Josie could not pick out her own mother and father. They were too far away and the sun was too bright.

Josie found the asparagus patch. "See, Maria, there is plenty." But though Maria squatted down and looked hard, she could not see the green spears hiding in the tall green grass.

Josie handed her a paper bag. "Sit down with this. I will pick them and you may put them inside the bag."

They were busy gathering and did not hear Mr. Curtis walk to the edge of the road and look down where they knelt on the ditch bank. "Well," he rumbled, "seems we have two minds with but a single thought."

Josie stood up. "Oh, I am sorry. Am I taking the asparagus from you?"

Mr. Curtis laughed. "No, what grows wild

33

is on a first come, first serve basis. There's plenty for both of us, I imagine."

When Josie had gathered all there was, she climbed back to the road and dropped some of the fresh spears into the pan Mr. Curtis carried.

"Thank you, girl. Season's almost over so we'll have to let the rest grow up and make seed for next year." He stooped to check Carlos' lip. "You're all looking healthy. No more accidents, I see."

Josie said, "No, sir."

They stood then on the road, awkwardly, unable to think of anything to say. Finally Mr. Curtis said gruffly, "Well, come on, let's walk back to my place. I haven't had breakfast yet. You can all have some milk and cookies while I have my eggs."

Josie grinned and turned the children toward the farm. Talking with him again would be much better than going back to their empty kitchen.

While the kettle boiled for Mr. Curtis' coffee, he took them on a tour of the house. Josie liked best the big upstairs bedroom that had been Janny's. Janny was Mr. Curtis' grown-up daughter. The room was bright and airy, its two windows opened to the morning. Outside the robins and starlings could be heard arguing over nesting rights in the maple trees. Photographs from Janny's high school years covered the walls. It was a room where a little girl had grown up into a woman. It was not like her own small room under the eaves where only a picture torn from a magazine hung on a nail.

"Forty-five years Mary and I lived here. It's been a good home. Still is." He dusted off Janny's graduation picture with his shirt sleeve. "Just the evenings sometimes get lonely. Did you ever notice that, Josie? In the summer around twilight, how mournful the croak of the frogs and the call of the night-birds?"

Josie nodded. Yes, she knew. And she could have told him of the loneliness of the Gulf shore and of the desert. It is people who keep back loneliness, she thought, wherever you are.

Mr. Curtis relished his skillet of bacon and eggs. He sopped up the egg yolks with huge bites of bread. When he had finished, he rubbed his hands down his pants legs and sighed, "Only thing I've learned to cook right. So eat my fill every morning and hope for the best the rest of the day."

Josie dried dishes as Mr. Curtis washed them. When they finished, he said, "I've got to see to some repairs on my fruit stand before I open it for the summer. Got time to stay and hand me my tools?"

Josie nodded.

"You'll have to be sharp. Janny used to be the best tool-hander there was."

Josie grinned. "I'll try."

Mr. Curtis had laid his hammer, nails, saw, and a few pieces of patch lumber out and was investigating the winter damage to his fruit stand, when they heard the clanging rattle of farm machinery on the road. As they glanced up from their work, a big tractor sputtered to a stop in front of them. The man driving looked at all of them and then spoke to Mr. Curtis.

"Hey, Curtis. See you're getting ready for another season."

Mr. Curtis nodded brusquely.

"Thought maybe this year you'd retire to your front porch and watch the rest of us work."

"Retire, Roy Welter? Why? So's you can have my farm?"

Josie thought, So this is Mr. Welter that Father and Mother work for. She had not met him before.

Mr. Welter swung himself down off the tractor. "Come on, you can't blame a guy for keeping his eyes open for a good piece of land."

"You had your eye on a good many pieces. Everyone in the neighborhood's sold out and gone, but me."

"It's a free country. I've a right to buy up the little farms to make one big one."

Josie held a board in place and Mr. Curtis nailed it fast with hard whacks of his hammer. "Did you ever think, Roy, that you get these farms from people when they're down on their luck?"

"Look, you know as well as I do that kids nowadays grow up and leave the farm. Your own daughter did. They go to the city where there's work. What's wrong with my taking these farms off the old people's hands, so they can retire to a senior citizen apartment and enjoy their old age?"

Mr. Curtis stared hard at Mr. Welter. "Roy, you were a boy right here. You remember what it used to be like. Neighbors. People working together. Helping each other when there was trouble, not waiting to gain from another's downfall. Now look at it. Farm buildings no longer being used. Houses cut into summer apartments for your workers and left to weather empty all winter." He pointed to Maria and Carlos, and Josie looked at the ground away from Mr. Welter's gaze. "Kids without supervision."

Roy Welter turned abruptly and stepped back on his tractor. "Times have changed since you were young. Even since I was a boy. People don't keep to themselves in neighborhoods anymore. They travel around. They don't stay tied to an apple orchard." He started up the tractor. "Whose kids are these anyway?" he called down.

"Name of García. People you've got put up on the old Miller place."

"They giving you trouble?"

"No, we are *neighbors,* you know."

"García is OK. Ramón proved himself last year at a tomato farm north of here. I hired him to come in with the early ones to help with the planting and cultivating. His wife can outpick a lot of men, I've been told."

Mr. Curtis wiped his sleeve across his sweaty face. "Seems to me she's needed home with her young ones."

"Mexican kids? They're used to running wild."

"You bring 'em here. They should be your responsibility. Roy, you can't take without putting back. It's nature's law." He turned away and then turned back. "Ought to have a nursery or something."

38

Roy Welter revved up the tractor motor. His laugh could be heard above the roar. "Don't get to be a do-gooder in your old age, Curtis."

They watched the tractor move off down the road. Its big tires, too wide for the narrow road, bit deep ruts in the grass on either side. By summer the road would be broken and muddied. The township would come by and patch it, but the heavy machinery would only break it through again.

Mr. Curtis sighed.

Josie watched as he let his eyes wander over the landscape before bending back to his work. "Look, Josie, fields as far as you can see, no trees, just fields." He pointed to his own corner farm, his shade trees, his orchard, his flowers and let his hand fall in despair. Even to Josie it seemed like such a little bit of beauty against the treeless landscape.

Mr. Curtis finished his patching and began putting his tools back into their carrier; then he stopped. "How about that broken step at your house? I almost tripped on it the other day carrying Maria. Someone ought to do something about it." He muttered, "Roy Welter sure won't be troubling himself over repairs. Not when he's letting all the buildings on the farms he buys rot down."

39

As they got near the house, they saw the line of diapers Josie had hung out earlier.

"Been busy as a bee I see."

Josie nodded, "Carlos, he always makes the washing."

Mr. Curtis spread out his tools again. "You little ones stay out of the way."

Maria and Carlos squatted wide-eyed until Josie sat down nearby and pulled Carlos onto her lap.

Mr. Curtis glanced at her over the tops of his bifocals. "You're quite a little mother, Josie. How long have you been taking care of the children?"

Josie shrugged her shoulders. "So long I do not remember not doing it. Mostly only the summers though. In the winter the work is not so plentiful. Then I go to school part of the time, and Mother stays with Maria and Carlos."

"You don't mind?"

Josie felt a pain inside of her as the thought of the other night came to her mind. The night she had caused her parents to fight. She said softly, "Mother is the one who works hard. I only do a little."

Mr. Curtis stopped his pounding and looked at Josie. "You're all right, girl. Kind of remind me of Janny when she was your age.

40

Janny used to stay right with me in the orchard. Like I said, handing me things, helping out. Sure missed her when she left."

"She does not live near here?"

"No, she went away to college, got married. They live in Rochester, New York now. She plays the organ there at one of the big churches."

"That sounds nice."

"It is, I suppose. We all gotta do what we like, I guess. Take you, Josie. What do you want to do when you grow up?"

"Nothing," Josie said softly.

"Come on now, every girl has dreams. Don't be ashamed of your dreams, Josie."

Josie could not answer this. Tears were running down her face and making damp stains on Carlos' undershirt, and she did not want Mr. Curtis to know that she was such a baby.

At the silence Mr. Curtis glanced up from his work. When he saw the tears, he moved to Josie. Letting his stiff leg hang down to the step he was fixing, his strong arms lifted both Josie and Carlos onto his lap.

Josie forgot she was twelve years old and almost in junior high school. She buried her head in Mr. Curtis' warm shoulder and let the tears continue falling. He said nothing, only let his hands pat a soothing rhythm on her shoulder.

When at last she lay silent, he said gruffly, but tenderly, "What did I say wrong, girl?"

With quiet sobs breaking the sentences into bits, Josie told Mr. Curtis her dream to stay in one place, to go to school, to someday be a teacher. She told him of the fight. "They work hard. They try so hard. And I hurt them."

Mr. Curtis cleared his throat several times before he spoke. "It's never wrong to seek something better, Josie. I'm not saying you didn't hurt your parents. You probably did. We parents have a way of getting hurt when we can't do all for our children we would like to do. But your wish isn't unreasonable. It's what young people want. A home. A future."

As Josie raised her head from Mr. Curtis' shoulder, she saw his eyes fill with sadness as they had that other day. He murmured, "It's what old folks want too. A secure home. A future."

He was quiet a long time. Then he roused himself to point to the southwest. "Right over there, Josie, used to be a big woods of oak, ash, and maple. Hickory trees, too. They're what brought the squirrels. I used to hunt them in the fall. Janny, Mary, and I picked

42

sponge mushrooms there in the spring." He pointed to the other side of the house. "Over there was a pear orchard. Just some old, scraggly trees, but always full of sweet Bartletts. And there, on back by the creek, another woods. That one was filled with dogwood. The whole thing pink and white with blossoms in the spring. Prettiest thing you've ever seen.

"We had neighbors in all these houses around. Kids, grown-ups, everybody used to get together for baseball in my corner pasture on a Sunday afternoon. Mary quilted with the women. We got together for bellings after weddings. Those were good times, Josie. Good times." His hand trembled as it rubbed his face.

Josie shyly interrupted, "What is a belling?"

"Never heard of a belling? Well, when a couple used to get married, all the neighbors would sneak down to their house at night with bells, horns, pans, and spoons and surround the house. Then at the same time we'd all start making noise. Kept it up till the newlyweds turned on the lights and came out on the porch. They always acted surprised, but inside was always cakes and pies and sandwiches."

Josie grinned.

Mr. Curtis grinned back, but then he sobered. "All gone now. Neighbors moved away. Kids grown. Old friends passed on. Small farm don't pay anymore, they say. People want too much, I guess. Not content with a few comforts, they want to own everything.

"Leastwise Roy Welter buys everything. One farm after another. Bulldozes the woods down. Takes out all the fence rows where the pheasants and rabbits live, so there's nothing but fields and more fields. He says he doesn't want anything standing in the way of his big machinery. Can't afford to turn out around woods and thickets. Bigger yield, that's his slogan.

"I'm the last one. I hang onto my handful of quietness, but I feel the fields closing in. He's waitin'. One day those bulldozers are going to get my place, Josie. I'm just a fogey, Roy Welter thinks. Just an old man in his way." He patted Josie one more time and set her back on the step.

As Josie watched him bend awkwardly over his job because of his stiff leg, she realized that she wasn't the only one to have a dream. Maybe Mr. Curtis did not understand how it was to always be going to a new school. Maybe he did not know how it was to be stared at when you said your name was Josie García.

Maybe he did not know the hurt of standing alone on the playground because you did not have a friend. But he did know what it was like to be afraid. Because he, too, was afraid of not having a place to belong. In this way they were alike.

She stood up. "You will stay for lunch, please?"

Mr. Curtis had his memories tamped back into place by this time. He looked up at Josie with a smile. "That would be nice. I want to see if you're a better cook than I am. I can't seem to get the hang of much except fried eggs."

Josie hurried inside to search the cupboards for something to feed her guest. From outside she heard the monotonous pounding of the hammer. "A handful of quietness," Mr. Curtis had said. What a nice thought that was. And it seemed right for the way he felt about his farm. She looked down at her hands holding a pan and a can of beans. "Will there be a handful of quietness for me?"

4

Ramón and Eva stood on the porch. The June sun gently touched the dew-wet grass, causing diamonds of light to glisten in the cool morning. But both of them knew the falseness of summer mornings. As beautiful as it was now, by ten o'clock the rays would not be gentle, but burning darts of heat that would cause sweat to drip into their eyes.

Eva looked at the repaired step and smiled at Josie as she joined them. "Your friend, Mr. Curtis, he fixes good."

Josie nodded, happy that her friend had been the one to please her mother.

Eva turned to Ramón. "It is a good job, eh, Ramón?"

Ramón grunted.

"Can you not say yes?"

Ramón scowled at Eva and Josie. "Yes, *Sí,* Eva, the old man does a good job fixing steps. You are happy now?"

Eva clucked her tongue and shook her head. "Men, you are all so jealous. You think you have to do everything yourselves. You do not know how to accept kindnesses."

Ramón's face scowled even more. "You have said enough in front of Josie, Eva. Come on, we will be late for work."

"What is the work for today?"

"Mr. Welter says we begin the first cultivation of tomatoes. I will drive the tractor. You will follow after the cultivator to see if I disturb any plants."

Eva shook her finger at her husband. "You drive careful then, Ramón, so I have no work. You get to looking at the other women working and you drive crooked. Then I break my back in the sun." She smiled to show him her scolding was in fun.

Ramón's bad temper passed as it always did under Eva's smile. He reached back and patted Eva's jeans where her hips made the pants fit snugly. "*Señora,* I think you can use the exercise of stooping." He brushed her hair with a kiss. "And I look at no woman but you."

Laughing softly, they took hands like young lovers, and Josie watched them with a smile as they walked down the road to begin another day's work.

At the main farm buildings workers were running in every direction. The pickles were coming into blossom, and this morning the bees Mr. Welter had rented for the pollinating had arrived on flatbed trucks. Roy Welter didn't have time to be a bee keeper and a vegetable farmer too, so he depended on bee farmers to supply him with the needed hives each summer when pollinating time came. Because it was so important to his crops, he was impatient this morning with his workers. His orders sent them scurrying. "Get these bees loaded. Remember no bees, no pollination; no pollination, no pickles; no pickles means no paychecks for any of us."

As soon as he saw the Garcías he called out, "Ramón, lend a hand. Load eight hives on the pickup and you and Raúl take them to the fields in the southwest square. Go 'round by the north road so you come up on the west end. Then get back here, and we'll load the bees for the northeast section."

Eva joined the knot of women who stood talking under the shade of the big oak. Roy Welter spotted them and called, "You women, get the files and sharpen the hoes while you wait. You'll be following the cultivators as soon as we distribute the bees. No use your wasting time."

The women did not complain. Sharpening hoes was nothing to bending in the fields. They could sit and catch up on one another's news. Usually they were too tired by the end of the day to do more than bid each other a tired *adiós*.

Like all mothers they began the conversation with talk of their children. Eva spoke proudly of Josie. "So quick to learn she is. I show her just once a job, and she remembers how to do it."

One old woman with coarse wrinkled skin and white straggly hair nodded her head. "You speak right to boast of Josie. You are a lucky woman. My children all grow up now and leave me to be alone. They quit school and run the streets in the city. So filled with hate they seem to be. My Juan, in jail now for a knife fight. Always the hot temper. They think we are treated unfairly. I tell them that may be, but to fight is not the answer. You are right, Eva, to praise God for such a girl as Josie." She shook her head and clucked her tongue, "So many go bad."

The other women murmured their agreement. But even as Eva felt warm with this praise, she also felt cold in her blood. Would Josie stay a good girl?

Since they were late getting into the fields, it was almost dark when they quit for the day. Ramón had driven the cultivator straight, but even so, many of the plants had to be straightened and patted back into the ground so their roots would not be exposed. Eva dragged tired feet slowly through the grass by the road as they walked home.

At the corner, Eva saw someone sitting on Mr. Curtis' front porch. "Ramón," she whispered, "that must be Josie's friend."

Ramón grunted a tired sound that meant merely that he had heard what she said.

They walked a few steps closer. "Do you think we should stop and say *gracias* for his helping?"

"We should not bother, I think."

"But is it a bother to say thank you?"

They rounded the corner.

"Do as you like, Eva. I will go home."

With those words Ramón walked faster and left Eva standing alone, undecided as to what to do. As she hesitated she heard a voice from behind the shrubbery say, "Mrs. García, why don't you come up on the porch a minute? I think it's time we got to know each other."

50

Eva rubbed dirty hands down the sides of her jeans and tried to scuff some of the dirt from her shoes. She did not want to track on this man's porch. He met her at the steps, his hand held out in greeting. She pulled hers back with the apology, "My hand, it is not clean for shaking."

"Nonsense, you think mine stay clean? I work outside too, you know." With a smile he took her hand and invited her to the swing. Eva blushed under this gentlemanly treatment.

"My husband and I want to thank you for your help to us and to our children."

"My pleasure. An old man gets lonely. My own grandchildren are too far away to visit often. And it takes children around to make a person feel happy. Don't you agree?"

Eva nodded. "Oh, yes."

"Take your Josie. She's quite a young lady. And smart as a whip."

Eva nodded again, more shyly with the praise.

"Tells me she wants to be a teacher."

Eva glanced at Mr. Curtis. He looked back at her and an unspoken understanding passed between them. "Excuse an old man's nosiness. But are you going to be able to do anything about it?"

51

Worry clouded Eva's dark eyes. "I do not know. There is no money, of course. And our moving, it is bad for going to school."

Mr. Curtis patted her hand and started the swing swaying. "Well, don't worry yet. You have time. And young people who want something bad enough seek to find a way to get it.

"Mrs. García, while I'm being a nosy neighbor, let me ask something else. Doesn't Josie have a friend her age?"

"No, she has few ways to meet other children. This summer we are here. When school starts, she stays maybe a month and moves on. The same will be true at the next school." She looked at Mr. Curtis. "You understand. It is easier if there is no one to leave behind."

"Perhaps. But perhaps the days of having a friend would soothe the pain of losing one. She needs someone to play with. Someone to be young with. I'm her friend, but an old man like me can't fill the need of a girl to talk to another girl about girl things. I was thinking of Roy Welter's daughter, Lydia. She's Josie's age."

"Mr. Welter's daughter?"

"Yes, she's kind of stuck out here in the country too. I'd like to have a party and get the two of 'em together. If you say yes, I

52

would be glad to watch the little children while the girls are busy with each other."

Eva looked doubtfully at Mr. Curtis. "It would not be too much trouble?"

"No. My parties come from the grocery store. Soda pop and potato chips."

"But Mr. Welter . . ."

"I'm thinking it might do both girls some good. Lydia could use some of Josie's good manners."

"You do what you think is best. If you think . . ."

"I think."

She stood up. "I go. Already supper is late for the baby. And we eat together."

Eva went down the steps and back to the road. The twilight was soft about her. She looked back once to wave at Mr. Curtis, where he sat alone watching her go. Her rest on the swing had been brief, but the tiredness in her body and mind had gone. Something had happened there to fill her with peace.

Soon, through the apple trees she saw the yellow light from her own kitchen window. Maybe she could not give everything she wanted to give to Josie, but perhaps she could help her to have this friend. She said a quick prayer, *"Dios asist . . .* God help."

5

Mr. Curtis lost no time in planning the party. He called on Josie and invited her. He saw Lydia riding by on her bicycle and asked her too. Lydia showed reluctance, but he talked on and on about Josie and the children, about the lunch he was serving, and about the girls being friends. He counted on two things, Lydia's usual curiosity and the shortage of girls her age to be with to share girl things. As a last bribe he added, "Josie even has a bike. You'll have someone to ride with."

"Well, OK," she had finally agreed, and then pedaled off quickly to show him she was only coming as a favor to him.

With the lie of the bicycle, the food for the party took second place in Mr. Curtis' mind.

Josie did not have a bicycle, of course, but Janny's old one was stored in the dusty, unused granary in the barn. It had been covered with burlap bags for years so he hadn't seen it, but it should be in good condition.

With a flashlight to show up the cobwebs before he walked into them, he unlatched the granary door and stepped in. It took a big heave to lift the bicycle over the high threshold and out into the light, but once out on the barn floor, it rolled on its own wheels. The daylight showed two flat tires, the rubber long ago hardened and cracked from neglect, and one pedal missing along with one handlebar grip. Rust speckled the chrome trim. Mr. Curtis shook his head and hurried back to the house as fast as his stiff leg would let him. He changed his everyday shirt for a clean, yellow sport shirt, picked up his wallet, and left for town. He had to get the hot dogs, colas, and potato chips anyway. While he was there, he'd just stop at the hardware store and get a few things for the bicycle. Nothing special, of course; just enough to get it running.

It had been a long time since Mr. Curtis had paid any attention to bicycle parts. He couldn't believe the displays. "Color coordinated," the clerk called it. "Everything to match."

"What do you know about that," Mr. Curtis marveled.

When he left the hardware store, he was struggling with a big package that contained red handlebar grips with silver flecks shining inside the plastic, matching pedals, and a matching banana seat. Over his shoulder were slung two tires, red like the other things. The clerk had even thrown in free red handlebar streamers. He showed Mr. Curtis how they slid into the handlebar grips and hung down.

"Real sporty," Mr. Curtis had answered. "Reminds me of when we hung squirrel tails on our car antennas when we wanted to impress the ladies."

Back home he was soon in the barn with screwdrivers and wrenches spread out around the crippled bike. Before he dared put on any of the pretties, he had to clean the gears with solvent and apply new oil. He tightened the spokes. Then, with steel wool and paste wax, he rubbed every bit of chrome until it was free from rust and shone like new.

When it was assembled, he stood back proudly and admired the silver and red beauty. "Good as new. Yes, sir. Good as new." Then he wheeled it to the edge of the barn. That evening he would present it to Josie.

The Garcías had finished eating when Mr. Curtis limped down the road pushing the bicycle beside him. Josie stood when she saw him coming, the rest of the family sat silently.

"Hello there," he called out. "Nice evening."

Eva smiled. Ramón nodded his head briefly.

"I was looking around in the barn today and came across Janny's old bicycle. Thought maybe you would like it, Josie."

Before Josie could speak, Ramón stood up, his hands jammed into the back pockets of his jeans. "No, thank you. The Garcías do not take charity."

"Who said anything about charity. It's a gift."

Ramón stood firm. "No."

"Why not?"

"If Josie has a bicycle, I will buy it for her."

"That's crazy . . ."

Ramón took a step forward and Eva reached for his arm. "Please, Mr. Curtis, you have done enough. We do not want to be a bother."

"I see." Mr. Curtis looked from Eva to Josie to Ramón. "Well, would you have any objections to Josie having it on loan, if she helps me in the stand in return?"

Ramón looked at Mr. Curtis, at Josie, at the bicycle. Josie's eyes were full of pleading. "You are sure there is work? This is not just a clever way you have of getting your own way?"

Mr. Curtis grinned. "You're sharp, García. I guarantee you there is work."

Ramón turned to Josie. "You want this job and this bicycle?"

Josie nodded.

Ramón held out his hand. "All right, agreed. But it is only a loan."

Josie tried to hug both men at once. "Thank you, Father. Thank you, Mr. Curtis. May I try it now?"

Mr. Curtis shook his head. "I'm sorry, Josie. I noticed coming down here the handlebars need tightening. I wouldn't want you to fall. I'll take it back with me, and tomorrow after the party you and Lydia can take it out for the first time."

When Mr. Curtis left, Ramón said to Eva, "It is not good for a bicycle to sit around unused. Mechanical things should be used. You know, Eva."

Eva took his hand. "I know."

Josie got up earlier than usual the next day, not sure whether it was excitement or nerves.

Either way, there was still the regular work to do before she could get dressed and go to the Curtis house for the lunch party.

At breakfast her mother reminded her of her manners and wished her a good time. Her father had scowled and said, "You make mistake, Eva. It is not right our Josie goes to a *partido* with Mr. Welter's daughter. Mr. Welter will say, 'Ramón, who do you think you are?' and I will lose my job."

Eva laid a gentle hand on Ramón's arm.

Ramón had said no more, but his grouchy face told both Eva and Josie he did not give his approval.

When the clock said eleven, Josie was beginning to think her father was right. How could she meet this girl? How would they talk? It would be like at school. She would be stared at. Someone different. But still she wanted to please Mr. Curtis. She knew he was doing this for her. The least she could do was go and be polite. Let this Lydia decide if they would be friends. Probably she would not want to, and then it would be Lydia who hurt Mr. Curtis, not her.

Carlos and Maria were scrubbed and dressed in clean shorts and T-shirts. Josie set them on the living-room couch with the warning, "You stay clean."

59

Then she washed herself and put on one of her school dresses that she had not worn since the last day of school in Florida. She brushed her hair, divided the shiny strands, and quickly braided them into tight long braids. When she could think of no more excuses, she gathered Carlos from the couch and took Maria's hand. "Come, we go now."

Mr. Curtis met them at the barn, and they had one look at the bicycle before they went to the house.

A few minutes later, as Josie watched from the kitchen window, she saw a girl, who must be Lydia, ride into the yard. She swung her leg over and jumped off her bike while it was still moving. She let it drop, not even looking back to see if it landed safely. Josie also saw that Lydia had worn white sneakers, a pair of cutoffs, and a white sweatshirt. As she bounded onto the porch in unladylike leaps, Josie felt self-conscious and out of place in her school dress, shoes, and socks. She had thought Lydia would wear a party dress and she would look plain. Now she realized it was she who was overdressed. It was only a neighborhood lunch after all. Anyone would know that. She retreated to the far side of the kitchen, holding Carlos and Maria before her as protection.

60

If Mr. Curtis noticed her embarrassment, he didn't let on. He welcomed Lydia at the door with a tease. "Hi, Freckles. What are you doing this summer to get into trouble?"

Lydia had all the usual coloring that goes with freckles—red rust hair, blue eyes, and fair skin. Josie wondered if she also had red-haired temper.

"Hi, Mr. Curtis. Mom says to ask you how soon before the Transparents will be ready for picking."

"Tell her three weeks, two if the weather stays this hot."

That taken care of, there was a silence as the three black-haired children faced the one red-haired one.

Mr. Curtis brought Lydia across the room. "Lydia, I want you to meet some new friends of mine. Josie, Maria, and Carlos García."

"Buenos días," said Lydia.

"How do you do?" replied Josie.

Mr. Curtis covered the awkwardness with a laugh. "Now don't you girls go changing languages on me, or I won't remember who's who."

They sat down to lunch. Carlos begged for a sip of cola, choked on it, and Josie upset the glass trying to pat his back; but otherwise the meal passed without too much strain.

61

Mr. Curtis said, "We'll leave the dishes. I'll take Carlos and Maria out to the swing for their nap. You girls get acquainted."

Before Josie could protest, she found herself alone with Lydia. The girl looked at her for a long time and then asked, "What grade you going to be in?"

"Seventh."

"Me too. You'll probably have old Mrs. Hammond for homeroom. She's a big grouch. But I forgot. It doesn't really make any difference to you, does it? You'll only be here that first month."

Josie nodded.

"You're lucky. Always moving away before the teacher finds out how dumb you are in things. Or are you smart?"

Josie felt it would be wrong for her to say so soon that she got all A's, so she shook her head and said, "No, I am not smart."

"Mr. Curtis says you got a bike. Where is it?"

"In Mr. Curtis' barn."

"You keep it there?"

"No, Mr. Curtis just gave it to me today. I haven't taken it home yet."

Lydia grabbed the back of a chair like she couldn't believe her ears. "Old Curtis *gave* you a bicycle?"

"Not exactly. He is loaning it to me for the summer. In return, I help him in the fruit-stand. It was his daughter's."

Lydia let loose of the chair. "Oh, that old thing. Well, I guess it's better than nothing. Come on, let's go ride. Did you see my 10-speed racer?"

They rode down the north road. Josie had all she could do to keep the front wheel from wobbling so she would not fall. It had been a long time since she had been on a bike. The last time had been an old one two winters ago in California. All the kids in the camp shared it. She did not want to fall and scratch this one. She would have to be very careful since it was only hers on loan.

Lydia kept riding ahead, turning, circling her, pressing on her hand brakes, causing her wheels to lock and skid in the loose gravel. It all scared Josie. She wished she had taken her first ride alone.

Finally, they stopped at a culvert to rest. They lay their bikes in the grass and sat on the cement bridge with their legs over the side. They watched the water below them trickle through the big tile.

Lydia stuck a piece of grass between her teeth and stared at Josie.

Josie kept staring at the water. She was not

sure yet what this girl thought of her. She seemed to be friendly, but she also seemed to be looking at her as if she were some animal in the zoo. It made her uncomfortable.

Finally Lydia said, "On Thursdays we go to the park for an outdoor movie. They got a swimming pool and some rides there. You want to go with me?"

Josie started to say yes, but she remembered in time. "No, I cannot. I have to watch Maria and Carlos until my parents come in from the fields."

Lydia shrugged her shoulders. "Whatever you say. Come on, race you back to the corner."

Josie knew she had lost the race before they even started. While she was still getting her pedal up to push off, Lydia was already standing up, pumping down the road with such speed her red hair flew out behind.

Mr. Curtis called to them as they came into the yard. "You're going too fast for such a hot day. Come up here and we'll have a popsicle to cool off."

Lydia finished her treat first and flung the stick into the shrubbery. "Have to be going. Thanks for lunch." She looked once more at Josie. "If it's the money, we have a pass to the park. It wouldn't cost you anything."

64

When she had gone, Mr. Curtis had to be told what that meant. He answered, "Go, Josie. I'll watch the little ones. Lydia's right. They have a season pass and it doesn't matter how many go in on it. You'll like it."

Josie did not know. Things were moving very fast. A bicycle, a job, a party, a new friend, *and* an invitation to a movie in such a short time.

Mr. Curtis said, "You push the bike to your house. I'll bring Carlos and Maria."

Josie noticed Mr. Curtis limped more than usual and walked slower because of it. "Are you all right?"

He nodded. "Just that some days are better than others. It's my old age creepin' up, Josie. That's all."

Josie felt a twinge of shame. So much good was happening to her she had not thought of Mr. Curtis very much today. Yet it was because of him all the good things were happening. To make up for her selfishness she said, "Tomorrow I will come down and help you drag the rest of the brush from the orchard for burning. You should not try to do that heavy work alone."

"I'd appreciate it, girl."

That evening, washing the dishes with her mother, Josie shared her day.

66

Eva put a dab of soapsuds on the tip of Josie's nose. "Mr. Curtis is a real friend. Work hard for him. We can only pay back friendship by giving something of ourselves in return."

Josie bobbed her head in agreement and swiped the suds from her nose.

Eva said, "Hey, I thought you promised me a garden of yellow flowers. What has happened to this promise?"

"I forgot. So much happens. But tomorrow I will dig the dirt. We will still have marigolds."

6

The first days of July hurried by Josie in a rush of hot sunshine, hard work, and times of fun. So much to do. Smuggled in with the sunshine came two days of rain. On those days Josie's mother did not have to go to the fields, which meant less heavy work for Josie, special food on the table, and a comfortable lap for Maria and Carlos to curl on while their mother's soothing voice sang quieting songs in Spanish. Days of rain in the García house brought their own special rays of comfort.

Remembering her promise to her mother, Josie had taken the short-handled hoe and tried to hack into the packed down dirt by their front porch. Even though she worked all the afternoon, until sweat soaked her shirt back, she had only broken the hard crust.

Discouraged, she had thrown the hoe down in disgust. Nothing would ever grow there!

But the following day, Mr. Curtis had brought his garden cultivator. He tugged the starter rope until the engine caught and the tiller blades turned. In one hour the blades had done what Josie alone could not do.

When the soil had been turned fine and soft, Mr. Curtis had brought fertilizer and they had raked it in deep. Then came the plants. Sturdy and green, they were planted in holes wet with cups of water. Over it all they spread peat moss. "The ground will stay moist now, Josie. We won't have to be afraid of that hard choking crust."

Josie had beamed at their garden. "How soon will they bloom?"

"Depends on the weather and the care they get. Moving them this late in the summer has been a shock, but now that they're settled in a permanent home, they'll spruce up and concentrate on making buds."

In between jobs Josie rode the bicycle. At night she covered it with an old cotton blanket and leaned it against the house under the protection of the porch roof, just in case of rain. During the day Lydia would come by and they would take short rides down the road while the children napped. Even though

Lydia protested, Josie always came back quickly to make sure the children were safely sleeping.

But her favorite time to ride was just at twilight. When the hot sun had gone down and the tractors had shut off their monotonous hum for another day, when the trees stood quiet waiting for the night, she would ride alone. The rhythm of her pedaling set the tempo for her thinking. Summer would never end. This time summer would go on and on and on.

Taking Mr. Curtis' advice, she had gone to the park and to the movie with Lydia. Mrs. Welter had parked the car in the outdoor show field. The girls had promised to remember which row their car was in, then they had walked around the park. Josie had watched the swimmers as they splashed and yelled in the blue, chlorinated water. They had watched the ferris wheel turn, a cartwheel of red and white. The horses on the merry-go-round had nodded in time to the calliope music. Lydia had said, "Only babies go on these rides."

Josie had been glad because she had no money with her.

Lydia had treated her to a caramel sucker on a stick, expected to last through two car-

70

toons and the feature. When the title *Spencer's Mountain* had flashed on the screen, Lydia had complained, "This old thing? I've seen it on television a thousand times already."

Josie, who did not have a television set, thought the story of a large family living on a farm in the mountains a good one. She hid her tears from Lydia when the grandfather died and when the oldest boy left for college. Lydia only sighed, "How nauseating."

Josie had also gone with the Welters to the fireworks display on July fourth. Her parents had stayed home with the little ones. "The park is so close we will be able to see the rockets from the porch. Then the children can watch in their pajamas and go quickly to bed."

Afterwards, Josie wished she had stayed home. Lydia had been in a bad mood that evening. Nothing Josie had said had seemed to please her. When she had tried to be polite to one of Lydia's school friends, Lydia had scolded, "Don't be pushy, Josie García. Remember, you're only here because I was nice enough to ask you."

Josie could not understand Lydia when she acted this way. But other days Lydia laughed and was fun, so Josie tried to forget the bad times.

71

July hurried on and everyone seemed even busier. The pickle fields were watched closely. The two days of rain and the regular irrigation had turned the fields into strong green vines heavy with pickles almost ready for picking. Mr. Welter walked through the fields checking every few rows. He was waiting for the moment they reached number two size to order the pickers into the fields.

Josie's mother and father were ready with strong canvas gloves and long-sleeved shirts to protect them from the rough pickle leaves. But even so, Josie knew that as the pickles reached their peak, the gloves would be discarded so they could pick faster. Then her mother would come home with hands raw, sometimes bleeding. She would rub vaseline into the sores hoping to heal them somewhat before the next day's picking. But no one complained. Now the paychecks were bigger. They were paid for each basket they filled. The faster they worked, the more money would be put aside for days when there would be no work.

Mr. Curtis had opened his roadside fruit stand. His Transparent apples were ripe. Customers bought them by the bushel to make into pies and quarts of applesauce to be put up for winter. Often Josie, Maria, and

72

Carlos walked down past the orchard to the shade of the stand. While the children played, she helped Mr. Curtis wait on trade.

Then came the day Josie was sure she would always remember. The afternoon was bright and clear with just enough breeze to cool the sun's heat. Mr. Curtis said, "Too nice a day to waste. Help me shut up the stand; we're going on a picnic."

They packed bottles of cold ginger ale and packages of hot dogs and marshmallows into a picnic basket and took them down the road a half a dozen miles to the river. In the shade of the willows, they put down a blanket and gathered driftwood for a bonfire. While the fire burned down, Mr. Curtis baited a hook for Maria and threw the line into a shallow pool where bluegills swam. The fish were too small to take a hook, but Maria laughed with excitement when she looked into the clear water and watched them nibble at the piece of hot-dog bun pressed tightly on her hook.

Josie ran here and there after Carlos as he toddled from one bit of trouble to the next. When the coals were red hot, they roasted the hot dogs and toasted the marshmallows. Worn-out and full, Carlos lay on the blanket and sucked his bottle until his eyes closed in sleep.

Watching the moving water of the river, Mr. Curtis said, "I used to come here fishing with Janny when she was your age. But she always did more eating than fishing. We'd sit here and watch the sun go down. When it was dark, we'd build up the fire to keep the mosquitoes away and watch the orange reflection bounce on the tiny waves. It's one of the few places around here that's still pretty much like it used to be."

Josie trailed a stick in the water watching the current separate and come together again on the other side.

"Ever notice how fast a river moves, Josie? Hurrying, always hurrying away, eager to get to somewhere around the next bend."

"Always moving, like some people," Josie said softly.

He stopped poking the fire. "Still troubled over moving on, Josie?"

She nodded. "This has been the best summer of my life. I do not want it to end."

"Maybe what's around the next bend will be better, Josie. We shouldn't be so content with what is that we don't look ahead."

Josie threw the stick into the water and stood up. "If you believed that, Mr. Curtis, you would not mind leaving your orchard and moving on yourself. But you know this is

74

the best place for you. You do not fool me with your words. One place is good for me, too." Tears filled her dark eyes.

Seeing them, Mr. Curtis stood up and put his arm around the girl's defiant shoulders. "All right, girl, all right. Then let's both make use of the time left us. Come on, I'll show you where there are some black raspberries ripe. You can surprise your mother and daddy with shortcake for supper tonight."

They found the bushes and filled Mr. Curtis' straw hat with the berries. There were so many that they also filled the empty hot-dog bun bag, the tray of the picnic basket and Maria's continually empty mouth. They saw a bullfrog on a sunken tree stump, a rabbit hopping through the tall grass, and a cardinal sitting on a slender branch of a fallen tree. When Mr. Curtis pointed out the red bird, he said, "See a cardinal, Josie, and you'll see your boyfriend before sundown. How about it, you got a boyfriend?"

She grinned, "Yes, I am with him today."

The next day Josie told Lydia about the picnic and fishing trip. Lydia tossed her head and said, "He's only good to you because you're so poor. He feels sorry for you." Then she got on her bike and rode home.

The words hurt, but Josie did not have long to worry about them, because that night someone crept up on their porch and stole the bicycle. Her father discovered it gone when he left the house to go to work.

"This is what happens when you get into debt to others. Now I will have to buy a bicycle or pay Mr. Curtis for the loss of this one. We will not be here long enough for you to work out the cost. You should listen to your father, Josie. Nothing is free. Do you see that now?"

"Yes, Father."

With reluctant feet Josie walked toward Mr. Curtis' house. Her mother had agreed that they would pay for the bicycle somehow. "I'll stay with the little ones, Josie, while you go tell Mr. Curtis," she said.

Josie knew it wasn't the bicycle itself that was important to Mr. Curtis. It was because it was something of Janny's. It was part of his memories when his family was with him and he was happy. How could she tell him she had been so careless?

But Mr. Curtis' first reaction was not sadness; it was anger. The anger was not for Josie, but for whoever would steal a bicycle from a little girl. He immediately set out for Roy Welter's. Even with his stiff leg, Josie had a difficult time keeping up.

76

Welter was in the barn, getting down baskets to take out to the fields. Without stopping, he said, "Glenn, come back tonight."

But Mr. Curtis set his mouth firm and straight. His blue eyes held no warmth, only coldness. "No, Welter. You find my girl's bicycle now. You know who stole it. You bring in these migrants, shove 'em in a dirty camp and forget 'em. You don't care what happens to them or anyone else. It's me who has to put up with their thieving. First my apples, now my girl's bicycle. Get it back. It's time you take some responsibility for what you're doing around here. There's something more to being a person than just gettin' what you want yourself and forgetting other folks and their wants. Maybe I am only a small-time farmer, but I got rights too. Just because you've decided to buy up the whole county doesn't make you a king."

Roy turned from where he stood in the loft and glared down at Mr. Curtis. "That's enough, old man."

The sound of Welter's voice made the workers stop working and listen. At first they had smiled, as Roy Welter had, at this blustery old man, but now they felt the tension.

"You've had your say. Now get back down on your corner patch of dirt and stay there.

I've got me a crop to harvest. I'll look into your bicycle complaint. And if I can't find it, I'll personally give you ten dollars to replace the piece of junk. But right now, get off my place. I've got work to do."

As Mr. Curtis and Josie walked across the yard, Josie heard Mr. Welter shout behind them, "Hey, Raúl, that the García kid?"

"*Sí.*"

The next words made Josie stop and turn to Mr. Curtis, fear in her eyes.

"Tell Ramón to see me tonight when he comes in from the field. His daughter is giving me a headache."

Mr. Curtis gripped Josie's hand. They walked slowly, Josie matching Mr. Curtis' limp. "Greed does bad things to a man, Josie. Look, as far as you can see—the Welter kingdom. Five big barns and the beginnings of a sixth. Over there, the bulldozers are leveling another thicket for another ten acres to plant. Enough will never be enough for Roy. He'll always want just a few more fields. He's so busy getting, he has no time for living."

But Josie was not listening. She was hearing Mr. Welter's voice again. Because of her, her father would be in trouble. How would she tell her mother when she got home? Her feet dragged, postponing what had to be.

7

Josie's sunshiny summer world shattered. Everything so right one day and so completely wrong the next. The sad day had ended with her father coming home, his head down, his forehead creased with worry.

"Mr. Welter says I receive warning. If I want to continue my job, I am to see my family does not cause any more trouble in the neighborhood. He says if we cannot live outside the camp, he will move us into camp where he can keep his eye on us." He had sat down heavily on the kitchen chair. "And Josie, you are no longer to see Mr. Welter's daughter. He says he does not approve of his family mixing with the workers." He had then slumped forward, his head in his hands.

"Your friend, Mr. Curtis, is nothing but a meddling old fool. A troublemaker."

Her mother had said, "Maybe this is an opportunity, Ramón. Maybe you should find a job that cannot be ended because an old man and your boss have a quarrel. Maybe the time is now to begin a new way. What do you think, eh, Ramón?"

Her father, already confused, had left the kitchen to get away from the question and the sound of more trouble. Josie had watched him walk to the nearest field, stoop down and pull a weed, check a plant, and pick a first ripe tomato for their table. She had felt miserable that any word or mistake of hers had caused him to walk with such heavy feet and bowed head.

Now, this morning Josie noticed, as she knelt by the marigolds, that even the flowers were not doing well. Most of them sagged limp in the July heat, even though she had watered them only last night. Feeling her work was useless, she put away the hoe and decided to visit Mr. Curtis. Maybe he could help her sort out this puzzle of things gone wrong.

By this time, Carlos and Maria knew where the walk down the road took them, so they ran ahead anxious to see their friend too.

Josie knocked at the door, but there was no answer. She could see his car in the drive, but he was not in the fruit stand or the yard. Why did he not answer? She knocked again. Then she noticed breakfast dishes still sitting on the table. Mr. Curtis never left the house until he had cleared away his breakfast dishes. He always left the kitchen clean "like Mary used to."

Cautiously, Josie opened the door and stepped in. She called, "Mr. Curtis?" Then a little louder, "Mr. Curtis?"

There was an answer from the living room. "Josie, girl? I'm in here."

Josie took the children's hands and they walked carefully into the quiet, carpeted living room. They did not often go in this part of the house. The draperies were drawn so it was dusky. They stood still while their eyes forgot the bright sunshine outside and adjusted to the gloom.

As things came into focus, she saw Mr. Curtis lying on his back on the couch. Without turning his head he held out his hand for her to come closer.

She moved to the couch. "Are you sick?"

"It's my stomach. When I get riled, my stomach kicks up. Should have known better than to lose my temper yesterday with Roy. It wasn't worth it. And then I should have known better than to have bacon and coffee this morning for breakfast. Don't set good."

"What can I do?"

"First thing, look in the medicine chest for a box of pills. The doctor gave 'em to me to settle the storms. And a glass of milk to take 'em with."

Josie ran to get the medicine and milk. After he took them, she went back to the kitchen and washed up the few dishes. She also picked up yesterday's newspaper and added it to the pile on the back porch. Maybe if he did not have to worry about the housework, his stomach would settle quicker.

When she had finished all the jobs she could see needed doing, she went back to the living room and dropped to her knees on the floor by Mr. Curtis. "You are feeling better?"

He nodded. "I'll just lay here till things get back to normal." He held out his hand over the side of the couch. She took it in both of hers. On the wall she noticed a picture that was sewn with bright thread. Part of it was what Mr. Curtis had said that day he had fixed the step, "Better is a handful of quietness than two hands full of toil and a striving after wind."

Mr. Curtis had seen where she was looking.

"You like Mary's sampler? She embroidered it a long time ago to pretty up the living room."

Josie nodded. "It is beautiful. What is its meaning?"

Mr. Curtis studied the ceiling. "Well, it's from the Bible. Book of Ecclesiastes. It's a part of a group of verses that I like. I admit I'm not educated and maybe I'm wrong, but to me it means, 'Glenn, be happy with what you got. Enjoy it. Don't be looking at other people and wanting what's theirs.'

"Another verse goes on about having a friend. How two can help each other." He squeezed her hand. "Kinda like us, I guess." Then he sighed, "I also have got to remember it says 'Better is a poor and wise youth than an old and foolish king.' I shouldn't have spouted off yesterday like I did." He closed his eyes, "God has something for all of us, Josie. We each just have to search for our own handful of quietness."

Josie looked at his tired, wrinkled face. She felt fear. He seemed so helpless and alone. She could not burden him with her problem. She would have to find her own answers. She stood to leave. "I will go now. I just came down to tell you I would look for the bicycle along the road. Perhaps someone took it only for a ride. Perhaps it is not really stolen, but laying forgotten somewhere."

"Don't you fret about it, honey. Don't make any difference."

With a promise to come back with supper for her patient, Josie took the children and started back home. She walked slowly, her mind so filled with questions that she did not hear Lydia ride up until she heard the crunch of gravel as Lydia slid her tires in her usual careless way.

Josie did not speak. Remembering how sad her father had looked last night, she would not speak first. Mr. Welter would not again accuse her of "associating" with his daughter.

"Hi. Where you been?"

"To see Mr. Curtis. He is not feeling well."

"Yesterday too much for him? Dad said he acted like a real maniac."

"He was upset over losing Janny's bicycle."

"It seems to me it was *you* who lost it, not him."

Josie squeezed the children's hands to keep from getting angry. "I mean he was upset that it was gone."

"Anyway, I bet he's sorry he ever took up with you now."

Josie could not hide her surprise. "Why?"

"Oh, nothing. It's just he takes you all over,

85

gives you all kind of things, and all you do for him is get him into trouble."

Josie knew Lydia was enjoying her shock, but she could not conceal it.

Had she really been only trouble to this man who had been kind to her? She wished it was not the peak of the harvest. She wished it was already fall, and they could get in their truck and ride away from this place. Why had she ever thought she would want to live here? Why had she ever thought having friends would be pleasant? They brought only pain in your heart. Crossly, she jerked Maria and Carlos after her down the road. "Hurry up, you bad children. You make me late to get the supper."

The children, unused to Josie in a bad temper, whimpered fretfully as they tried to trot their short legs fast enough to keep up with Josie's longer angry strides.

8

It was the first week in August. Josie now knew there was no one to help her solve the mystery of the bicycle. Mr. Curtis stayed sick, unable to get outside even to the orchard. He fretted about his harvest, just beginning, and the fretting only made his stomach worse. Her mother and father were picking tomatoes now, and if they had any spare hours, they searched the pickle fields for the last of the pickles. Every filled basket was more money and more security. Often they came home so late they had only enough energy to pour the warm water Josie had ready into the basin, wash the field dust from their bodies, tousle the hair of the little children, and fall wearily into bed.

Josie was busy herself. She tended her garden, which still looked straggly, did her housework and took Maria and Carlos with her and opened Mr. Curtis' stand for him in the afternoons. She liked sitting in the cool shade of the stand. The quiet was comfortable. Only enough customers stopped to keep the hours from being monotonous. The only thing she did not like was Lydia's riding by every day, stopping long enough to take an apple from one of the baskets and ask, "Found your bike yet?"

One bright hot day, Josie was sitting at the stand as usual. And as usual her thoughts thumbed through the summer, searching for the reason why everything had gone wrong, when she touched a thought that made her sit straight on her little stool. Why did Lydia keep asking about the bicycle? Why was she so interested? She is like someone who knows a secret and cannot keep from bringing up the subject.

Since there had not been a customer for the last hour, Josie closed the stand and hurried home. Quickly she put the children into their beds for a nap, then she stood at the upstairs window where she could watch the road. For once, Josie was thankful Mr. Welter had cut all the trees. From her high window she could see clearly in all directions. And just as she knew would happen, in about a half an hour, Lydia came riding down the road. She turned and stopped in front of the closed stand. She looked around, then rode back to the corner and pedaled down the north road. When she was almost out of sight, Josie saw her get off her bicycle and slide down the ditch bank. In a few minutes she scrambled back up to the road, threw her leg over her bike, and rode off toward home.

Josie thought, What is down that road? Then she remembered. The concrete culvert. The big tile under the road. The place they had rested the day she had gotten her bike. "Tonight," she whispered to herself, "when Mother and Father are home to watch the children, I am going to find out what is so interesting in the culvert."

Supper dragged by for Josie. She was anxious for everyone to finish eating so she could quickly wash the dishes. Her mother put the children to bed and, after apologizing to Josie for being too tired to stay up and talk to her, also went to bed. Josie picked up a magazine so her parents would think she was going to read. Instead, she sat quietly in the living room waiting for the boards overhead to stop creaking. When all was still, she felt safe to get the flashlight and tiptoe out the door and down the porch steps into the dark night. Carefully she felt her way. She did not want to trip or fall and have to explain what she was doing.

When her feet found the blacktop of the road, she began running. She used the flashlight only for emergencies. It would not do to have a telltale light making a trail in the darkness.

All lights at the Curtis house were out. She slowed to a fast walk as she crossed the bridge at the crossroads and turned north. Once she left the protection of the orchard and walked between the long flat fields, she felt a shiver of fear. She did not like walking alone in the dark even though there was some moonlight. The way seemed farther than it had this afternoon as she watched from her window.

She tried not to think of the darkness. Only when she thought she had gone almost far enough did she turn on the flashlight. The weak yellow beam darted up and down until it picked up the culvert. Josie left the road and carefully felt her way down the ditch bank. As she stooped at the entrance of the large tile she thought, I hope no animal has chosen this place for his bedroom tonight.

Taking a deep breath, she peered into the dark tunnel. Her flashlight flicked over the hole. It was as she suspected. There, half in the mud and half leaning against the tile, was her bicycle. It didn't look much like it had the day Mr. Curtis had loaned it to her. Its red tires were mud splattered. The chrome trim had patches of rust growing, the handlebars were twisted. Josie groaned and the groan echoed inside the hollow pipe.

She took a step to rescue the bicycle when she thought, If I leave it here, Lydia will come back to check on it. I will wait and catch her. Then let her explain how she knows such a secret. As Lydia had earlier that afternoon, Josie scrambled up the bank leaving the bicycle still hidden.

Josie's feet flew as she started back home. The bicycle was found! None of the migrants were thieves! Mr. Curtis would no longer be worried! Each step seemed to stamp out another of her problems. It had been a worthwhile hunt.

Back in her bed, she soon fell asleep.

The next morning Josie tried to do two tasks at once to finish her work more quickly. She sang as she worked, and Maria and Carlos were happy to have their sister herself again. They played contentedly on the floor while she finished the ironing. As she hung away the last workshirt of her father's, she said, "Put away the toys. We are going to Mr. Curtis' house."

The children needed no further reward to make them obey. Quickly the blocks and wooden clothespins were dropped into the cardboard box, and they were ready to go.

Mr. Curtis was up and sitting on the porch when they came skipping across the yard. "It does me good to see three smiling children," he greeted them. "What's happened? Someone declare Christmas in August?"

Josie shook her head, "No, but I will have a surprise for you this afternoon, I think. Do you feel well enough to watch Carlos and Maria for me?"

"Sure, but what's this mystery?"

"I cannot tell you yet."

Mr. Curtis gathered the little children up on either side of him and pretended to be angry at Josie. "All right, keep your secrets. Go on, go away. We'll just sit here and have us a story." He looked down at Maria, "Do you know why mamas and daddies call their babies honey?"

Solemnly Maria shook her head.

"You don't? Well, I'll tell you this story about the little baby, the big bear, and the honey tree. It used to be one of Janny's favorites. 'Once upon a time in the deep dark

92

forest lived a mommy and a daddy and their little baby, too. Now that mommy loved that daddy . . ."

As Josie ran down the steps and around the house, Mr. Curtis' voice faded away. She had decided to stay off the north road. She would go through the back of the orchard. When she reached the fields, she would have to crouch down to stay hidden. It would take longer, but she did not want to be discovered. Besides she had plenty of time. Lydia usually did not come by until midafternoon, and it was only one-thirty now.

She managed to arrive at the culvert with only dirt on her knees and a thistle scratch on her right arm. Looking quickly up and down the road, she stood up long enough to jump the ditch; then she hid inside the culvert. The ground squished under her tennis shoes, so she inched herself along until she reached a fairly large, flat stone. It proved big enough for her to sit on and still keep her feet drawn up out of the mud and water. She settled down to wait.

She soon found it not a pleasant occupation. As the afternoon got hotter, the culvert got stuffy. The ditch water smelled stagnant, and a swarm of gnats flew against her face. Before long her legs cramped, and when a small garter snake slithered by, she almost gave up her plan altogether.

But just when the waiting became almost unbearable, she heard a crunch on the gravel road above her. It was too light to be a car. It had to be Lydia's bicycle.

She held her breath.

A shadow blacked out the daylight and Josie waited. Lydia must not have been able to see her crouched there in the dim tunnel, because she only looked toward the bicycle and then straightened as though to leave.

Josie stood up and called out, "Good afternoon, Lydia."

Lydia jumped and almost fell into the muddy ditch water. "Who . . . who's there?"

Josie walked quickly out into the bright sunlight, forgetting about keeping her feet dry. "Are you looking for something?"

Lydia's face turned so pale the freckles seemed to spatter paint her face in contrast. Then she turned to run.

But she could not struggle up the bank quickly enough to escape Josie. Josie reached the road as soon as Lydia did and put her hand on Lydia's bicycle to keep her from running away. "I think you have something to say to me."

"You leave me be, Josie García. I haven't

any time for you," Lydia struggled. "I have to go to the tomato field to tell the men to bring the truck to the barn for unloading. My father is waiting."

"Then he will keep waiting. You are not going anywhere until you explain to me why you took my bicycle."

"I don't have to tell you anything. You dumb migrant."

Josie showed some anger of her own by grabbing a handful of Lydia's tangled red hair. "You call me no names. I am as good as you are, Lydia Welter. Better. I do not steal bicycles and I do not steal apples. I will not let you make me feel poor anymore."

Lydia's hands found Josie's black braids. "Why should I steal your old bicycle when I have a ten speed myself?"

"Because you are a spiteful, bad girl. You are jealous."

"Jealous of you? You make me laugh."

Both girls were so busy fighting they did not hear the car drive up until Mr. Welter was out and yelling, "Lydia, I sent you on an errand. Why have you kept me waiting?"

Both girls dropped their arms and stepped back.

Mr. Welter turned to Josie and grabbed her shoulder. "What is the meaning of your

96

fighting with my daughter? Weren't you told to keep away from her?"

Josie stared defiantly at Mr. Welter, but spoke to Lydia. "Tell him, Lydia."

Mr. Welter tightened his hold. "Don't you worry about Lydia. I'm talking to you."

"If you do not tell him, Lydia, I will."

Lydia doubled up her fist behind her father's back, "You do and you'll be sorry, Josie García."

With the realization that something important was wrong, Roy relaxed his grip and turned to his daughter. "What's going on here, Lydia?"

"Nothing. She's just trying to get me into trouble."

"What are you two doing down here? Josie, what's your story?"

Josie continued to stare at Lydia. "I was looking for the bicycle Mr. Curtis loaned to me."

Roy looked at Lydia, then back at Josie. "And did you find it?"

"That's what I think you had better ask Lydia."

Roy said, "Well, Lydia?"

Lydia tried to continue her bluff, but she couldn't do it. Her face twisted as tears came to her eyes and she flung herself against her father. "It's all your fault. You made me do it."

"Made you do what?"

"Hide her old bicycle. I got so tired of hearing her talk about Mr. Curtis and her bicycle and her marigold garden and their fishing trip. She thinks she's so smart."

"But what does that have to do with me?"

"Mr. Curtis is not even her relative. You are my father and never take me anywhere. You're always too busy with your old tomatoes and pickles to notice me. Why should she have a friend and I have nobody for company?"

Roy held his daughter at arm's length for a few silent moments, then he stooped down and held her to him. This was more than he could straighten out in a few minutes. "No more now, Lydia. We'll talk about this at home." He looked over at Josie and said in a kinder voice this time, "Where is the bicycle?"

"In the culvert."

Roy patted Lydia one more time, then went down the bank to bring the bike out of the mud. When it was standing on the road, it was indeed a sorry sight. "I'll buy you a new one, Josie."

But Josie shook her head. "This was Janny's. It means a lot to Mr. Curtis."

98

Roy nodded, "I understand. I'll fix it up and repaint it."

As Lydia stood sulking, Roy Welter put the two bicycles in the trunk. Then he opened the car door and said, "Get in, Lydia." As he got in beside her Josie heard him say, "Lydia, how could you steal something that belongs to someone else? Haven't I taught you better than that?"

Josie watched the car speed down the narrow road. Then she turned and ran toward Mr. Curtis' house. To find the bicycle was like putting down Carlos after carrying him a long way. She could rest again.

It must have been the same for Mr. Curtis. When she had told him, he looked relieved and said, "Guess I better get to bed early tonight. Time I get to picking the Sweet Bows and the Wilson Reds. Say, how would you like to work more hours? This time for money. I have to have help picking."

Josie agreed.

9

Josie saw her mother leave the road and turn in their yard. She was alone. When Josie went to meet her, she said, "Mr. Welter wanted to see your father. Supper will have to wait."

"I know." Once again Josie told the story of the bicycle.

Josie's mother sat down and took Josie's hand in her own calloused one. "You are a good girl, Josie. So hard you work. So well you take care of the babies. And I can trust you to tell the truth, to do what is right. This Lydia has so much, but she does this bad thing. I do not understand."

Josie did not often say serious things to her mother. It made her embarrassed. But this time Josie leaned down and kissed the rough

100

hand holding hers and said, "Today Lydia said *I* have a friend and *she* has no one. I thought about all she has. I have something much more important than her 10-speed bicycle and fine house. I have love from you and Father and Mr. Curtis. That is all I really need." Quickly, she got up and stirred the soup on the stove, so she could pretend she did not see the tears glistening in her mother's eyes.

But she did hear a whispered, *"Gracias, Josie."*

Soon they heard the slow steps of Ramón coming up the walk. Eva poured warm water into the basin, so he could wash up quickly. He would be hungry after such a long day. But his face, when he came through the door, made her stop and put her hand to her throat in alarm. "What is it, Ramón?"

"I have quit my job."

Josie stopped dishing the soup. Even the little ones, sensing something wrong, stopped their playing. Eva could not believe what she heard. "You did what?"

"I quit my job." His chin jutted stubbornly as he looked at his family. "When this man comes to me and says, 'Ramón, forgive me for calling your daughter a troublemaker,' I think why did not this man listen to me before, when I try to tell him my daughter is good girl? No, then he only say, 'Ramón keep Josie away from my daughter.' And I remember how you say, Eva, maybe there is something better. A job where a man can be a man and not be ashamed. Then I also think of Josie and Maria and Carlos. They need to go to school so they do not grow up to be like you and me, afraid to speak what we know is true, afraid we will lose our job. They need to be trained. And when I think all these things, I say, 'Mr. Welter I will stay until this harvest is in, because I would not leave anyone with a crop in the field. But then I no longer work for you. I do not want to follow the crops anymore."

Eva looked afraid, but then she quickly looked proud. She went to Ramón. "You did the right thing. We have the money we save to travel. Now we will use it to live while you find a job."

Josie served the soup. As they ate, she stared at hers. She had forced her father to fight. What would happen now? But even as she worried, a thought of happiness punched its way into her mind. *She was going to go to school in one school.* She was not going to move on. Tomorrow she would tell Mr. Curtis this good news.

But then the worry edged back in and pushed the happy thought aside. Was it such good news? Where would Father find another job? It seemed her worries had not ended with finding her bicycle.

10

As the days of August slipped by, Josie found herself too busy to worry about what might lie beyond September and the opening of school. Her mother arose even earlier in the morning, and together they did the housework because Josie had to spend more hours in the orchard. She picked apples for Mr. Curtis while Maria and Carlos played in the soft grass beneath the trees. The early apples hung sweet and ripe, and without moving from one spot, she often filled her canvas picking bag to the top. Mr. Curtis had pruned the trees well, so they bent down making tall ladders in the orchard useless. Only the very top apples required climbing to reach. She convinced Mr. Curtis she liked climbing, so he stayed on the ground looking up while she stretched and pulled the apples from the topmost limbs. She was glad that she could do this for him. She was afraid if he climbed, his stiff leg would become tangled in the branches, and he would fall.

When the sun got too hot, they loaded the apples on a flatbed trailer, hitched the small tractor to it, and pulled the fruit to the shade of the barn. During the afternoon and evening, customers lined the drive and roadside as they purchased bushels of the fruit, often calling, "How soon before you'll have cider, Glenn?" Josie knew the two months ahead would be even busier. When the Delicious and Jonathan started ripening, Mr. Curtis would have to hire more pickers. But for now, they managed to keep up.

In the evenings Josie searched in her closet for last year's school dresses. Some of them she lengthened, but others were too tight in the shoulders and had to be put away for Maria to grow into someday. Her mother told her she could buy new clothes for school with the money she was earning.

With all of these things to do, she had no time to notice that Lydia no longer rode by on her bicycle. Also, she did not notice the worry frowns on her father's face as the pickle crop ended, and only a few tomatoes were left.

Ramón, however, was counting the days. He had not yet found a job. Very soon the hot August days would turn to September. There would be fields to turn under with the plow, but Ramón knew he would not be the one to get this extra work. Mr. Welter had ignored him since the day he had said he would quit, except to give him the hard, dirty jobs no one wanted. No, when the tomatoes were finished, he must have another job. Josie would be in school, Maria in kindergarten. Eva would be needed at home to care for Carlos. The weather would become cold. They would need warm winter clothes, coal for the stove in the living room. The living room! They would not even have that if they did not find another house to move to. They could not stay on in the house when his job was over with Mr. Welter.

Whenever there was rain or an off day from picking, Ramón would climb into the rattly truck and continue his job hunting. He could not work in a factory running a machine. He did not know how. And all of the personnel managers said, "You must have experience."

He could not take a job bagging groceries at the market. He needed more money than they paid.

106

He went to the park, but the park manager said, "We close in the fall, and there will be no jobs here until we open next spring. People do not like to go to amusement parks in cold weather."

Each day he came home discouraged. It was only Eva's soft voice that kept him trying. She always believed he could do whatever he decided to do. She encouraged him to do his best, much the same way she quietly urged Josie and Maria and Carlos to do their best. It was her faith that gave him any hope of doing this impossible thing he had set out to do. He could not let her down.

One day he drove fifteen miles to the town where Mr. Welter sold his produce. He thought he might find work in the cannery. But the man there shook his head. "We're just finishing our busy season. We'll be cutting back now. Only those with seniority will stay through the year. Sorry."

Ramón murmured his thanks and had turned to go when the man called after him. "Why not try the appliance factory? They might need someone on the line."

So Ramón drove to the factory and with almost no hope presented himself at the desk of yet another man in charge of hiring. He was so discouraged that he did not immediately believe his ears when the man said, "Yes, we do have an opening."

Ramón was so surprised he said, "One with no experience needed?"

The man laughed. "No experience needed. Come on, I'll show you."

Ramón followed the man out of the office and down a long hall that opened into the factory. When the door opened, Ramón could not believe the noise that hit him. The machines banged and hummed and rattled. People stood with blank faces before a moving belt and tightened a screw, or added a part, or inspected a finished product. When they did talk to one another, they had to shout above the noise of the machinery.

They walked on through the factory until the man tapped Ramón on the shoulder. "Here," he shouted, "is what you will do."

A young man was standing at the end of the assembly line of washing machines. As each machine came by him he lifted the lid, picked up a free box of detergent, placed it inside the machine, and closed the lid. Ramón watched as the man lifted, stooped, placed, closed. Then again, lift . . . stoop . . . place . . . close.

"This is all I would do?"

"That's all. Think you could handle it?"

Ramón nodded.

They went back to the office and discussed salary and starting time. "The young man you saw working will be quitting to go back to college soon. It was only a summer job for him. You will replace him. OK?"

Ramón agreed.

On the way home Ramón thought about the job. The pay was better than he was now making in the fields. That was good. It was steady. That was good. It was inside, out of the hot sun, cold wind, and rain. They could stay now. There would be money. The job was easy. He could do it. All this was good, was it not? Then why was he not happier? Was it the noise of the factory after the quiet of the outdoors? Surely he could get used to that. Other people did. Was it the routine of the job? Many jobs were routine. He would be getting paid for doing one thing. If he did that well, he would have no problems. No worries at night. No decisions to make.

He looked into the rearview mirror of the truck and told himself, "Ramón, you are lucky man. You needed a job. You have a job. They pay you big money. It is better than moving from camp to camp. Better than having a boss who can say, 'Ramón, keep your family away from mine.' Go home then, Ramón. Tell Eva the news."

Eva had supper on the table as he came in. He smelled the *enchiladas* as he came through the door. Putting a smile on his face, he took a deep breath and called out. "Eva, children. Come, I tell you the news."

Eva's hand flew to her throat. "You have a job."

Ramón threw up his hands. "You do not even let a man tell his own news!"

Eva ran to him and covered his face with kisses. "Oh, Ramón."

"Tell us, Father."

"Only after I have eaten. Your supper smells too good."

While he helped himself to the dish of *tortillas* covered with steaming tomatoes, peppers, onions and cheese, he knew the others were waiting. So after a few mouthfuls, he began to describe to them his job at the factory. "It is making washing machines."

Eva's breath was a long "ohhhh?"

"Yes. You see, we all stand in a line and every person does just one thing. That way the machine moves faster. Everyone's job is important, because without each person, we would not have a complete machine."

Eva's eyes filled with pride. "And you can do work like this? You can do your share building this machine?"

110

Ramón looked away from her proud eyes. He busied himself with another bite of food. "*Sí*, Eva. I have my job like the others."

Josie asked, "What is your part, Father?"

Ramón looked around at all of his family. How could he say to them, "I put the soap box inside." They would be ashamed. Better they did not know. Better it be only his shame. He would tell a small lie. "I cannot explain it to you, Josie. It is too hard for you to understand. You would have to see it."

Ramón finished his meal quickly and walked out to the yard. Better he told that lie. Now Eva could tell the other women with pride, "My Ramón works on an assembly line in a factory." She would not have to make apologies to the other women, "He puts soap boxes inside."

He walked about the yard picking up bits of sticks and paper. He looked at the bare yard and sagging fence. He knelt by Josie's marigold garden. The soil was dry. Perhaps if he watered them, the tiny buds that were starting would somehow manage to bloom. He went around back and got the scrub bucket and pumped it full of water. With an empty soup can, he carefully dipped a canful from the bucket and placed it close to the plant where it would soak down and water the roots of the flowers. As he worked over the growing plants, the memory of the noisy factory faded. It was almost dark before he went back into the house to Eva and the children.

11

The first day of school Josie and Maria were both up before the sun topped the apple orchard. Maria, who would not be five until the next week, seemed too much a baby to be going to kindergarten thought Josie. But Maria did not think so. She talked eagerly about what she would learn. She checked again and again to see if her crayons and tablet were ready.

Josie felt, since she was older, she should try to hold her excitement inside. But this was a new school, maybe the last new school she would ever have to attend, and it was the first year of junior high. Because of her picking apples, she was better dressed for the beginning of school than she had ever been before. Her red plaid skirt and red blouse made her

114

black hair seem shinier and blacker. She carried a new notebook and several pens and pencils.

Eva stood by, watching both the breakfast and her two girls. With the ending of the tomato crop, she had been able to quit before Ramón and stay home with Carlos.

Josie was already watching the road for the bus, when she saw Mr. Curtis hurrying toward the house. He came out, "Josie!"

She met him on the front porch. "Why are you out so early?"

"Got presents for my girls." To Maria he held out a Mickey Mouse pencil box and to Josie, a box tied with a ribbon. "Open it, girl."

Josie fumbled with the ribbon and box lid. Inside was cotton. She lifted the soft layer and underneath lay a tiny silver pennant. In red was the word TIGERS.

"It's your school nickname. All the kids wear them. I thought it would help you feel at home."

Josie hugged Mr. Curtis. "Thank you so much. Help me put it on, please."

With the pin in place, Mr. Curtis held Josie by the shoulders. "It will take more than a pin, won't it, Josie?"

Josie sobered. "Yes, but this is the last time. Just this one more time I will have to ignore their stares and teasing about my brown face and my Mexican name." Her chin raised. "But it is the last time. I know I can do it."

"Just let them know Josie as I know her, and you'll have no trouble making friends."

Mr. Curtis stepped back as they heard the bus lumbering down the road. The air brakes squealed. Eva called, *"Adiós,* my girls. Make me proud of you."

Mr. Curtis said, "I'll be waitin' to hear all about it tonight."

Josie lifted Maria up the two big steps into the bus and guided her down the aisle to an empty seat. She did not even know Lydia was in the seat behind them until she heard her voice, *"Buenos Días,* Josie García."

Josie heard several giggles. She would ignore them. She merely turned to Lydia and said, "Good morning, Lydia."

"How's the apple picking?"

Josie knew she could snap back an angry answer, but that was exactly what Lydia wanted so she simply shook her head.

The other conversations had stopped. The kids were watching the "new girl" getting initiated.

"Yes, I heard you were picking apples. Next year will you be joining your parents in *my* father's fields?"

Josie shut her mouth tight and held Maria's hand. Her past hurts had taught her not to answer taunts. It only made the teasing worse. All she could do was hold her head high and hope the bus soon reached the school.

Josie saw Maria safely to the kindergarten room, then climbed the stairs to the second floor where the junior high and high school had their rooms. For a country school it was big. Each grade was divided into three rooms of 35 or more students. The stairway monitor told her the A's through H's met in room 22. Josie was glad Welter began with a W; she would not be in Lydia's homeroom.

Contrary to Lydia's prediction, she did not get Mrs. Hammond for homeroom, but a new, young teacher named Miss Li Chang. A quick moving, smiling woman, she was originally from Hong Kong. She dipped her head to Josie in a slight bow and said in a lilting musical voice, "I'm pleased you have come to be with us, Josie García."

Josie found it easy to return the friendly smile. A little bit of her relaxed as she accepted the stiff white student's card and was told, "Take this to the principal, along with your records." Again the smile. "Besides being your homeroom teacher, I will also be

117

teaching you Home Economics. Maybe, with our Chinese and Mexican backgrounds, we can teach the other girls some interesting dishes this year."

Josie hurried away with the card. The sooner she got back, the sooner she could learn to know this new teacher better.

The office was hushed after the hubbub of the busy halls. Josie sat down in one of the wooden chairs. A boy was waiting and another girl. They both held white cards, so Josie knew they were also new students. Teachers came in and checked their mailboxes, smiled at the three, and left. The boy busied himself making an airplane out of his pencil, a pin, and his card. The girl, who was tiny with long, silky blonde hair and crystal blue green eyes, glanced up occasionally and smiled at Josie.

Finally Josie said during one of the glances, "My name is Josie García. What is yours?"

"Heather Davis. We moved here from near Detroit. Where are you from?"

Josie looked away from the unusual eyes and said, "No place. I mean we have always moved, following the crops. But no more. We are staying here. My father has a job on the assembly line of the appliance factory."

Heather smiled. "I'm glad you're staying.

118

Perhaps we can be friends. It's always easier in a new school if you have another new girl as first friend."

"You have moved before?"

"Oh, yes, lots of times. My father often is transferred. That's why I get good grades in Social Studies. I've been so many places. It always makes extra credit reports easier. I bet you do the same."

Josie said, "I never thought of that before, but you are right."

The day passed quickly. Josie reported to each of her classes. Lydia was only in her math class. But luckily, Heather was in her English class *and* Home Economics. Miss Chang let them choose each other for working partners on projects.

Miss Chang also told them she would be calling on their mothers for a home visit. "Because we will be doing home projects during the year, your mothers need to know how they can help their daughters."

Josie was still trying to learn her way in the maze of halls when the final bell rang to close her first day of school, and she was pushing right along with the others to get out the door to find a seat on the proper bus for the ride home.

At home she shared her day and then

119

asked, "May I go to Mr. Curtis' house? I want to tell him it was a good day."

"Yes, run away. You are too excited to help me anyway."

As Josie ran out the door, she saw taped to the cupboard the picture of a squirrel colored bright red that was Maria's first paper from school.

Mr. Curtis met Josie at the door with a plateful of cookies and two glasses of milk. "Saw you coming. Thought you'd like a snack on the porch while you tell me all about it."

They sat comfortably in the swing now. They were old friends.

Mr. Curtis had not been to the school since Janny had graduated, so he asked many questions about the new addition just opened this year and about the teachers, the new ones and the ones he remembered.

As their conversation began to run out, they saw Ramón across the road in the abandoned tomato field. He walked slowly, his head down. As they watched, he stepped carefully over the rows, even though they were past harvest. Sometimes he stopped to pull a big ragweed.

Mr. Curtis nodded toward Ramón. "Your dad still working for Welter?"

"Just until the end of the week."

120

"Then he goes to the factory?"

Josie nodded.

"How does he feel about his new job? Talk much about it?"

Josie frowned, trying to think. "He talked that first night. But no, he does not mention it since. But he is quiet. He does not talk much."

"Not a talker like me, eh, Josie?" They laughed and then Mr. Curtis stared across the field at the lonely man. "Better a handful of quietness . . ."

Josie wondered.

He reached over and patted her hand. "Run on home now and help your momma. Thanks for telling me about your day."

Josie walked off the porch. She looked over at her father. He had bent down. When he straightened, he held a round ripe tomato in his hand.

Then she glanced back at Mr. Curtis. He stood leaning against the rail of the porch, so the weight was off his bad leg. His mouth was partly open. He seemed excited.

12

Two days later, as Josie was getting her books from her locker to go home, Miss Chang walked over to her and asked, "Is your mother home today?"

Josie said yes.

"I would like to make my home visit at your house this afternoon. Would you like to ride with me instead of going on the bus?"

Josie agreed. While Miss Chang closed the windows of their room, Josie went by Maria's room for her, then they walked together to the teacher's parking lot. Miss Chang stopped by a bright, blue foreign car. "I hope you don't mind bouncing down the road in my bug."

Josie said, "It is better than our truck."

"How do you like our school, Josie?"

"Very much, thank you."

"Your records show you are a very good student. And this year I understand you are staying the full term."

"Yes, my father has a job in the factory."

"And what does your mother do?"

"Now she is staying home with my little brother. Always she has helped my father in the fields for the extra money."

As Miss Chang followed her directions to turn at the next road, Josie asked, "Is it very difficult to get into college?"

"You would like to go to college, Josie?"

"I want to teach little children. The kindergarten or first grade."

"Today with scholarships and student loans, if you keep your grades high, you should have no trouble. But you will have to work hard. This was how I got my education. That, plus working at a restaurant waiting tables for extra money."

Josie said, "Stop at the next house." And as they did, Josie saw their house as it must look to Miss Chang, and she felt ashamed of the run-down, sagging place. Quickly she said, "We have not lived here long and maybe we will move."

Miss Chang let the car bump to a halt in the ruts in front of the house. "Josie, I do not go to my students' homes to judge or criticize.

123

Make no apologies. With people it is what is inside that is important. You are a fine girl. There must be love inside your house."

Josie jumped out of the car taking Maria. She felt embarrassed listening to Miss Chang saying such serious things.

After Josie introduced Miss Chang to her mother, she went to the kitchen to fix two cups of coffee. She did not want to be in the room while they talked about her. It would not be polite to listen. But, perhaps she would overhear some words from the kitchen. That would not be the same as eavesdropping.

Miss Chang sat on one of the wooden straight chairs, her skirt pulled neatly to her knees. On her lap she opened a notebook. "Mrs. García, this year Josie will be expected to complete four home projects—two this semester, and two next. They are to be of her choosing; whatever interests her in the way of homemaking. Child care, cooking, sewing, cleaning. When Josie has completed a project, I will have a question-answer sheet for you to fill in. This is not a grade, but only to help Josie put into practice what she learns in the classroom. Do you understand?"

Eva had listened closely to the musical voice of the teacher, trying to understand what was expected of her. This would be important to

Josie. "*Sí*, I think I understand. But you see we have little to work with. No oven to bake in, no sewing machine to sew on. This will make a difference in grade for Josie?"

"No." Miss Chang looked at the bare windows. "Josie could help you make curtains. Handwork is acceptable."

Eva looked down at her rough, stained hands. Then she tried to hide them from the teacher in the folds of her skirt. "This school. It means much to Josie. She wants to go to college."

Eva's voice trembled with emotion, causing Miss Chang to leave her chair and go over and sit on the couch. She placed her small hand on one of Eva's rough ones. "Josie and I have talked. There are ways. Josie has a good record. And we will help her, you and I."

Miss Chang went back to her seat, closed her notebook, and zipped it shut just as Josie came in with the hot strong coffee. "That smells good, Josie. I like black coffee after my work. We don't drink tea all the time you know."

Miss Chang's joke ended the formal visit and they all felt more at ease. Miss Chang asked Eva, "Have you thought of a job, Mrs. García, now that you are leaving the fields?"

Eva said, "I have thought of it, but I do not

know of anything I could do. And there is Carlos to watch."

"But you would like to work?"

"*Sí*, I am used to being busy."

Miss Chang put down her coffee cup. "Maybe I should explain why I am asking. We need one more cook in the school cafeteria, and I have been looking for someone as I make my home visits. Would you be interested?"

"Work in Josie's school? Making lunch for the children?"

"Yes."

"*Sí*. That I would like. I would work hard."

"The head cook is a competent person. She handles her staff very well. I think you would like all of them."

"Oh, *sí*."

"And if you need some place for your baby, there is a day care center near the school. The charge is small. You could make arrangements."

Eva said again, "Thank you."

Miss Chang stood, "Then it's settled. I'll recommend you to the School Board. They will tell you your salary and when you will start to work." She held out her hand. "Goodbye, it was a pleasure meeting you."

Josie followed Miss Chang to her car.

126

"Thank you for the job for my mother. I know she wants to help my father by working."

"Josie, your mother is beautiful. She wants what is best for you."

Josie nodded. She watched the car bounce out of sight down the narrow road before walking back to the house. She stopped to look at her marigolds. Since the hot sun no longer beat down on them in the afternoon, they had begun to look stronger. They held themselves tall and healthy. But they had no blooms. She scolded them. "Why can you not make even one flower for me?"

In the kitchen her mother was already banging pans on the table as she sang. Her cheeks glowed like a young girl's. "Oh, Josie, do you suppose they wear white uniforms in the kitchen at your school?"

"Yes, they do."

"I will wear one too. I will make friends. I will be able to buy dishes for the table that match. And I will buy a pot of red geraniums like I see at the discount store."

As Josie watched her mother happily planning, she understood for the first time that her mother had also been lonely. Her mother had wanted to belong and to have friends, but she had never complained. She had gone to

127

the fields every morning, worked hard, but still had come home with a smile and a hug for each of them. Josie ran and threw her arms around her mother in a tight squeeze. "I am so glad you are my mother." And she felt her mother's arms tighten around her in return.

By the time Ramón came in for supper, the house was alive with gaiety. They all tried to outtalk the others in telling their father the news of Eva's possible job. Finally he held his hands over his ears in dismay. *"Quieto!* One at a time, you talk. Your mother first."

Eva, her eyes shiny black with eagerness told Ramón Miss Chang's offer. "You see, Ramón. We both work. We make so much money, we have no worries here. We make friends. We go to the stores and to the church. People will say, 'Good morning, Mr. and Mrs. García. How are you today?' And when there is no school, I will be home with the children. The job is *perfecto."*

Ramón patted Eva's shoulder. "Yes, Eva. If this is what you want. The job for you is *perfecto."*

Eva kissed Ramón. "And other good news. Josie's teacher says Josie is a smart girl. Are you proud of your daughter?"

Ramón included Josie in the embrace. "I am proud of all of my family. No matter what, I will do what I can to please you." Then he sat down to the table to eat.

But some of the happiness had left the room. Josie did not know how or where it had gone, but in its place had come a sadness that quieted their laughing.

Later, she looked from her bedroom window and saw her father across the road in the moonlit empty field. She saw him stop, pick up a handful of dirt, and let it run through his fingers as he stared across the land.

But Josie could not read her father's thoughts. She could not know that her freedom would be paid for by his imprisonment inside factory walls. But she did feel her father's slumped shoulders had something to do with the sadness that had come into the house at suppertime.

13

Saturday Josie took advantage of her day off from school to help Mr. Curtis pick up windfall apples for cider. The sun was warm, but where the apples hid in the long velvety grass, it felt cool and the air smelled of the mellow apples. They talked about Heather, who was proving to be stiff competition for Josie in class. And Josie also told Mr. Curtis about her first experience running the electric sewing machine in Home Economics class.

"Miss Chang said to push the lever just lightly, but I pushed too hard, and the machine went tearing along the material . . . zip. Miss Chang yelled, 'Stop pushing the lever, Josie,' but I was scared and pushed all the harder. Just before I got to the end of the

130

material, Miss Chang pulled the plug to the machine. I do not think I will ever be a seamstress."

Mr. Curtis was laughing, "No, I think you better choose a different career. Unless your customers . . ." A car door slamming interrupted. "Someone's in the driveway. Probably one of *my* customers. Your legs are younger, Josie. Run up and see if you can take care of whoever it is."

Josie put down her picking bag and ran toward the barn. Her feet slowed considerably when she recognized the car in the driveway. It was Mr. Welter's and Mr. Welter, himself, was just getting out. She stood at the edge of the trees, not sure what to do.

Welter glanced around, then saw Josie. "Guess you're the girl I want to see. I got your bike in the trunk. Curtis around?"

Josie nodded. "In the orchard."

"Will you get him while I unload the bike?"

Josie nodded again and sped off.

She felt braver returning with Mr. Curtis. When they walked out of the trees, the bicycle stood as shiny as it had been before Lydia had hidden it.

Mr. Curtis circled it looking closely at the tires and spokes. "You sure it's safe? I don't want Josie falling and hurting herself."

"It's safe. I had it completely overhauled." Welter looked down at the ground, "Guess that squares us."

But Mr. Curtis wasn't about to let Roy Welter off that easy. "You think repairing the bicycle your daughter broke is enough, do you? You don't have anything to say to my friend here?"

Josie wished he had not brought attention to her. But if Mr. Curtis was a fighter, so was Josie. She stood tall and looked Mr. Welter in the eye.

Mr. Welter said hesitantly, "I think you know, Josie, I'm real sorry about what happened. Lydia had no business doing such a crazy thing. I apologize for her."

Mr. Welter looked back at Mr. Curtis. "That satisfy you?"

"Not quite, Roy. What about the way you talked about Josie, about her not being good enough for your daughter and all? What about that?"

Mr. Welter's face was turning red. Josie thought he was like a schoolboy being scolded by his teacher. But he was holding his temper. "OK, you're a fine girl, Josie. I take back what I said."

Again he looked at Mr. Curtis. "Now?"

Mr. Curtis looked thoughtful. "Well, I

don't know. Seems you were doing a lot of spouting off back then." He looked hard at Welter.

"You mean that day in the barn?"

Mr. Curtis nodded.

"Well, Curtis, sometimes you can be darn aggravating."

"That's the privilege of old age."

Welter sighed, "So what do you want from me?"

Josie could tell by the way Mr. Curtis ran his hands down inside his back pockets and leaned back that this was just what he had been waiting for.

Mr. Curtis gestured with his head toward her house. "I was just thinking about the old Miller house."

Roy Welter looked suspicious. "What about it?"

"Going to let it set empty all winter?"

Welter nodded once, "I suppose."

Josie wondered what Mr. Curtis was thinking of. He knew that her father was no longer working for Mr. Welter and that they were trying to find another place.

"Seems to me a wise businessman like yourself could find a better use for his investment than letting it set idle eight months out of the year."

Welter moved restlessly. "I've got work to do. What are you getting at?"

"You asked me what I wanted from you. I want neighbors. I want the Garcías to stay on."

Josie saw Mr. Welter tighten his jaw muscles. "I can't afford charity."

"No one's asking you to. Charge them rent."

Josie held her breath in the silence. What if Mr. Welter lost his temper? What if there was a fight? But then she saw his jaw relax and his mouth twitch as if he were trying to hold back a smile. "Think you're pretty smart, don't you?"

"Known you all your life, Roy. Know you can't pass up a dollar."

Josie tried not to look too eager when Mr. Welter looked her way, but behind her back she crossed her fingers.

Welter turned back to Curtis. "Fifty dollars a month and they do their own fixing up."

"That's robbery for that old place. Forty dollars and you fix it up."

"Curtis, you are the darnedest busybody I've ever met. Forty-five and I'll furnish the paint."

Josie wanted to jump up and down and say yes, yes, yes, we will take it, but Curtis winked

135

at her and said, "We'll have to think about it. We'll let you know our decision before Monday."

Welter shook his head in disbelief at this unbusinesslike way of doing business. "Whatever you say. Don't mind me." He crawled into his car and drove away still shaking his head.

When he had turned at the crossroads, Josie said, "Let us go and tell my father right now."

But Mr. Curtis laid a hand on Josie's arm. "Not yet. I got a plan in mind. Let's get back and finish our job."

Josie obediently followed Mr. Curtis back into the orchard, but she could not keep her mind from wondering what plan Mr. Curtis could have. What could be more wonderful than their being able to stay on in their house and with paint to make it look like a real home. Maybe she would even master the electric sewing machine and *sew* curtains for the windows.

When they had piled all of the apples in the barn by the cider press, Mr. Curtis looked across the road and saw Ramón walking through the abandoned tomato field. Josie wanted to call to him, but Mr. Curtis shook his head and only watched the man stepping over the tangled vines, sometimes pulling a ragweed, sometimes bending and picking a small ripe tomato.

Finally he took Josie's hand, "Come on, girl. Let's have a talk with your dad."

They went down to the service bridge that crossed over into the field, and even though they did not walk quietly, Ramón was too deep in thought to hear them approach.

As they came up behind him, Josie said, "Father?"

Ramón looked around startled, "Josie, Mr. Curtis. Pardon, I did not know anyone was here."

Mr. Curtis came right to the point with his first question. "How much do you want this factory job?"

Ramón looked surprised. "I *need* the job very much for my family."

"That's not what I asked. I asked how much you *want* the job."

"It is a good job. Much money. Inside, where it will be warm this winter."

"Doggone it, man. Answer my question."

Josie, knowing her father's bad temper, thought, Why is Mr. Curtis trying to pick fights with everyone today?

Ramón glanced at Josie and then looked at

137

the ground. Mr. Curtis cleared his throat, "That's what I thought. You have to be around growing things just like I do. I thought I recognized in you the same love for the land."

Ramón raised his hands in silent pleading. Josie felt her heart jump to her throat and lodge there in a sob. What had she done to make her father leave what he loved best? Why had she not understood that his handful of quietness was different from hers?

Mr. Curtis turned and started back across the field. "Come on, you two, we're going to the house to talk business."

Ramón looked at Josie. Josie raised her eyebrows and shook her head. She did not know what Mr. Curtis was thinking about. To find out, they would have to follow.

Mr. Curtis tripped on a dying tomato vine, and Ramón gestured for Josie to catch up and hold on to his arm.

They did not speak until they were at the kitchen table in Mr. Curtis' house, and he had a stack of ledgers piled in front of them. Then he looked Ramón García in the eye and said soberly, "How would you like to run my orchard for me, starting this Monday?"

Ramón's face was blank with astonishment. "Run your orchard?"

"Yes, I can't do it anymore. Every year I have to let more of the work go. The trees don't get pruned properly. I can't get in the trees to pick. Josie could even see that. I try, but I'm getting too old, Ramón. Yet this is my life. I planted these trees when my daughter was just a baby. I raised 'em like I did her, tenderly, with love. Now she's moved away and Mary's gone. There's just me and the trees. I feel if I have to give up my trees, I've nothing to live for."

Ramón's eyes had begun to widen with interest, but he did not speak.

"I know it's a lot to ask of a neighbor, but I watched you out there, Ramón. You love the earth, the plants. They aren't just money to you, they're living things that need you. I saw myself in you, like I was when I was young with a family. Believe me, if I thought you wanted the factory job, I wouldn't have said anything to you. I would have kept my mouth shut and held out here until there was nothing else to do but let Welter buy me out and put me in a home. But I saw you and you're my hope of staying."

Ramón's mouth worked with emotion. "Mr. Curtis, I do not know what to say. This . . . this offer, it is like it is from heaven."

Glenn laughed, "Don't go giving me powers I don't have. I'm just a fogey old man who selfishly wants to live out his day on his own place. First, are you interested?"

"Of course!" Ramón, too, was laughing.

"Oh, Father," Josie cried and hugged him around the neck.

"Then let's look at these books, so you can get an idea of the financial arrangements."

Together they poured over the ledgers. "The last of the picking is early November. There's enough room in the barn to cold-storage apples all winter. If there are many small or deformed apples, I run the cider press until Christmas. That gives us only January and February as slack time to get our equipment in shape for the next season. Come March, you'll be out pruning. The more work you can do yourself, the more money you'll make. I'll be some help to you, and Josie too. We should only need pickers during the peak of the season. It's not a large business, but it supported my family and with you as a good manager, I think it can support yours. Since I've got the small tractor and cultivator, I suggest you use any spare ground for truck vegetables. I will have time to run the stand, and it will be more income if we add vegetables to the fruit."

Ramón did not interrupt the words. He

140

merely nodded now and then or murmured a quiet *sí* of understanding.

"Before you say a final yes, let me warn you this winter will be tight for both of us. Things are some run-down. My blasted arthritis kept me out of the trees this spring, and I didn't get done all I should. Do you have anything in reserve to see you through the beginning?"

Ramón, thinking of the money put away for travel and of Eva's new job, nodded his head.

"I've talked to Welter and you can stay next door. I'll pay the rent as part of your salary and a hundred a week until the next crop and then we go on a percentage basis. OK?"

Mr. Curtis held out his hand. Ramón took it in his own strong one and they shook on their deal.

"*Gracias,* Mr. Curtis. Go with Josie and me to tell Eva."

Together, they left the house. Instead of taking the road, Mr. Curtis led the way through the orchard. "Just to start getting you acquainted."

Eva was in the backyard hanging some clothes when the three trooped out of the orchard and stepped over the dividing fence. Josie ran ahead of the two men. "Momma, wait until you hear the news!"

141

Eva dried her hands on her apron and looked questioningly at Ramón.

"Sí, Eva." And because Ramón was so excited, he continued to speak in Spanish, and Mr. Curtis could not understand the conversation. But he knew by the look of disbelief, then amazement, and finally happiness on Eva's face that she was understanding and approving their plan.

When Ramón stopped talking, Eva walked over to Mr. Curtis and laid her hand on his cheek. "Thank you. You make all of us happy. Josie has her school, I have my new job at the cafeteria, for my Ramón this work with you, and a house where we will belong. You are a good friend. Come, you will stay to supper."

Mr. Curtis reached up and took the hand from his cheek and patted it. Josie thought she could see a tear glistening. "I'd appreciate it, Mrs. García."

As they walked around the corner of the house, Josie cried out. "Look, my flowers. They are blooming."

There, proudly, nodded the first yellow marigold. Other plants offered many buds just ready to burst open.

Mr. Curtis nodded, "See, Josie. Didn't I tell you marigolds would bloom for you? They're late, but they'll still have several weeks before frost."

"And I will have flower seeds to plant next spring." Josie put her hand into Mr. Curtis' as they climbed the porch steps.